T0208481

LIGHTNING

LIGHTNING

THE BEGINNING

SILVER FOX

LIGHTNING
THE BEGINNING

iUniverse books may be ordered through booksellers or by contacting:

iUniverse
1663 Liberty Drive
Bloomington, IN 47403
www.iuniverse.com
1-800-Authors (1-800-288-4677)

ISBN: 978-1-6632-0068-6 (sc)
ISBN: 978-1-6632-0069-3 (e)

Print information available on the last page.

iUniverse rev. date: 06/24/2020

CHAPTER ONE

MEETING MY FAMILY

Welcome to the Hunter family. There are four of us; my dad, Mark; my mom, Beth; my younger brother, Rocky; and me, Mickey. I am named after my dad's favorite baseball player Mickey Mantle, and Rocky was named after my father's favorite boxer Rocky Marciano. Both Rocky and I are tall for our ages. At 12-years-old, I am almost six feet tall and weigh 130 pounds, while Rocky is 7-years-old and already four-feet six-inches tall and weighs 85 pounds. My father is just over six-foot-seven inches tall with long blond hair that he keeps pulled back into a ponytail as a reminder of his Hippy Days.

My dad is one of the most relaxed people I know, and all those around him respect his sharp mind and broad shoulders. He had planned to become a lawyer all his life, but it wasn't until he graduated from Harvard Law School that he changed his mind and decided he wanted to do something in the field of business.

At his first interview after college, they offered my dad a management position at their company. On his first day at his new job, he met and fell in love with his secretary, my mother. They got married six months later. Then nine months later, I was born, and so here I am today.

My mom happens to be very, very tall for a lady, and like Dad, she is also mild-mannered and soft-spoken as well. I can easily say with certainty, and with confidence, she is very, very tall because she happens to be the tallest mom at my school. She is just over six-feet-one-inch. When they attend a function at school, she towers head and shoulders above the rest of the moms. When they travel to one of my football or basketball games, I never have any trouble finding her or Dad in the crowd as they both tower over the rest of the parents.

Mom has always worn her long blond hair pulled back into a ponytail, and it always reminded me of pictures that I have seen of Arabian horses with their tails arched up then cascading down their back legs. The way my mom wears it causes her hair to swish back and forth as she walks, just like an Arabian's tail.

And then finally, to top off the rest of our clan is my little brother Rocky. He also has blond hair, not unlike the rest of our family but, with one exception, his hair has a reddish tint to it. My mom calls his hair color strawberry blond.

I find my little brother, Rocky, is the world's most significant pest of all time. The main reason for our problems is because we share the same bedroom, and he is always getting into my stuff. But despite that, I love him anyway. Now I ask you who could not help but love their greatest admirer.

When I see some of my dad's school pictures when he was my age, I find both Rocky and I look just like Dad did at each grade level. We aren't only the tallest kids in our classes, but both Rocky and I are also the best athletes in our classes. Rocky and I both have many friends, and we're quite popular at school.

During their school days, both Mom and Dad were tops in their classes academically. Every year our parents are approached by our teachers who try to push them to move both of us to a higher grade level. The teachers used the test scores that placed both of us at a high genius level as their reason. Each teacher felt our current grade levels were holding us back and wasting our time and talents. But Mom and Dad were united in keeping us in our particular grade level we were supposed to be in for our ages. So, every year when asked to move us up to higher grade levels, their answer was always a quick and firm, "NO WAY!" We want our sons to have as normal a childhood as possible." And that was the end of that every time.

Enough about our family history because I want to move on to the good stuff.

CHAPTER TWO

COMING OF AGE

As I think back to just before the incident that changed my life forever, I remember I was a very happy camper that morning, because that day was my twelfth birthday. I pondered that morning on just how long it felt I had been eleven-years-old. It seemed to me that it had been for such a long, long time. I thought this was a right-of-passage, being one year closer to becoming a teenager, and in only four more years, I will be old enough to get my driver's license. I could hardly wait as I imagined myself being able to drive a car, and the freedom that will give me!

I grabbed a quick shower and then dressed quickly. After I finished dressing, I went back into the bathroom, brushed my teeth, and combed my hair. Then I paused for a second surveying the finished product. I decided that I was indeed ready to face the world at this the beginning of my twelfth year here on this earth. So I ran downstairs to have breakfast.

When I got downstairs, all the family was at the table and, not one of them had waited for me. I saw all three were at different stages of finishing breakfast. It was my birthday, so I felt they should have waited for me to get there to eat; that hurt my feelings. But then Mom placed my plate in front of me. I loved what I saw, and so all was forgiven. She had made my all-time favorite breakfast, and that pushed my feeling of disappointment away fast. I found that this special breakfast had made me feel special once again. My love for Mickey Mouse pancakes lifted my spirits. Mom had even put chocolate chips on the pancakes

3

to create the eyes, nose, and mouth of Mickey's face, and, as Mom knows, I like pancakes this way even better than chocolate cake. As she set the plate in front of me, I saw that not only was the Mickey Mouse pancakes all dressed up this way, but also on the plate were three strips of bacon. They were each fried up extra crispy just the way I liked my bacon cooked. Dad has always kidded me about my crispy bacon, saying, "Your bacon done that way is just short of the burnt offering stage." I found myself in seventh heaven; I just knew that this morning's beginning was the start of the very best birthday ever.

Mom reached over and gave me a big hug and said, "Happy Birthday Mickey!" Father echoed Mom's best wishes, then he reached into his shirt pocket and pulled something out. Without even looking at the object, he tossed it across the table; it bounced a couple of times and came to rest right in front of me. As I looked at it closer, I saw that it was a key.

I picked it up, looked at the key and, said jokingly, "Thanks, Dad, I always wanted a new Mustang." That made Dad chuckle, and Dad being Dad, was never slow with a quick response, "You never know." He paused, then finished with, "So right after you finish your breakfast, why don't you go out to the garage and see just what that key fits." My thoughts flashed to, "Maybe – he didn't say it wasn't a car."

I pushed back my chair and started to leave immediately. Mom stopped me and said, "Remember what your dad said to check after you finish your breakfast." She went on to state rather firmly, "I do need both of you two to hurry a bit because I do not want to miss your school buses, especially today." I sat back down, looked across at my father, who just nodded his approval of what my mom had just said, and with a wordless gesture, he pointed to my plate and smiled.

I could feel the excitement building, and I just knew that this pent-up excitement was making me about ready to pop. So I just started to eat faster and swallowing without thoroughly chewing my food. Dad frowned at me when he saw I was gulping down my food. Without even uttering a word, he dropped one side of the newspaper, and let it rest in his lap. Dad looked up and gestured to me by extending his right hand with his palm down, making a slow patting motion. I nodded yes to let Dad know that I understood what he meant, and that I was more than willing to do what he asks. I immediately slowed down my chewing of my food. Dad's smile of approval showed me he liked my follow-through, and he then went back to reading the newspaper.

It was only a few moments later that I cleaned my plate. I got my mom's attention and while nodding towards the empty plate, and I asked, "May I please be excused?" Mom looked at my plate and then at Dad nodding her head approvingly. I turned my attention towards Dad. He did not speak but just nodded yes after moving the newspaper aside, to see if my plate was indeed empty. He then folded the paper and rose to lead the rest of us towards the garage.

When I rose to go check my present, I paused long enough to tell my mom, "Thanks, Mom, for making my favorite breakfast."

She simply nodded her approval and said, "Thank you, Mickey, for being so polite."

After I thanked Mom and as I started to pass Rocky, I took special note of the limited space to get behind him. The amount of maple syrup covering his hands and face would ruin my school clothes if I got too close to him. I cleverly used my evasive skills of a great football quarterback trying to sidestep a rushing linebacker that I had learned. I found that I was able to sidestep those Icky Sticky Hands, and keep them at bay. As I was dodging those Icky Sticky Hands, I reached down and kissed him on the right cheek. You see, I knew that my little brother was a hugger. Knowing this, I had used my quick and cunning observations, I found the only syrup free place on his whole face. He reached up again to return my kiss, but I again dodged those Icky Sticky Hands. Rocky just said, "Happy Birthday, Mickey!"

I said, "Thanks, Rocky."

After the near-miss of the Icky Sticky Hands, I continued towards the garage to claim my Birthday gift.

I could hear Rocky sliding off the chair behind me. I listened to his feet hit the floor behind me, remembered those Icky Sticky Hands, and decided to pick up the pace a little. I opened the door to exit into the garage quickly. As the door swung open, I quickly glanced back and saw Mom to the rescue; she snagged Rocky's right arm just above the syrup line. She had waylaid him, and while steering him toward the kitchen sink, I saw Mom grab a washcloth and, with only three swipes, she very aptly wiped the Icky Sticky Hands and that syrupy face clean. I then saw her flip the used washcloth back in the sink with a great hook shot that would be the envy of any NBA Basketball Player making a thirty-foot hook shot.

I walked through the inner-garage door, following Dad, and I could hear the rest of the tribe following us. I was so excited I just knew this was going to be the very best birthday ever. I thought that I might know what my present was, but I did not want to say it out loud and jinx it. I knew there was always a chance I could be wrong. Another reason I did not want to say what I hoped for was because I did not want to hurt Mom's or Dad's feelings if they got a different gift for me. A new bike was high on my needs list but, my birthday was very close to Christmas, and the bicycle that I wanted cost almost five hundred dollars but, I could only hope as I walked forward.

I remembered the problems I had this summer. My two best friends had relatively new ten-speed trail bikes, and I had an excellent older ten-speed bike handed down from my dad bike that he had used while attending college. With it, I had always been able to keep up. I had always found more, often than not, that I would be the one leading the pack. We went just about everywhere on our bikes.

Then disaster struck, someone stole my bike! My buddies, Tommy and Billy, and I liked to go fishing way upriver for the bigger trout. The distance up to a couple of our secret places was quite a ride, but now it took us twice as long to get there. This problem was after I reported my bike as stolen, my buddy Tommy gave me his older fat-tired one-speed. My friends never complained about having to wait for me as I always fell behind them. I still felt that it had to be bugging them at least somewhat because it bugged me.

After six months, Sheriff Beau Dean had not been able to find a trace of my bike anywhere. So all summer long, I had to settle for the old fat-tired one-speed bike. But I was thankful for the use of it because, without it, I would have been afoot and would have been even slower, so I never complained about the bike.

As I walked towards the center of the garage, I was jolted back from my daydreaming to the present. I found that I could not see anything at first. But, after Dad flicked on all the lights in the garage, I could finally see it. In between Mom's and Dad's cars was the most beautiful shiny blue bike that I had ever seen in my whole life. I could see, even at this distance and with the dim light and shadows. As I stepped closer, I saw the bike had a chain with a plastic coating on each link so that it would not scratch the bike's paint. I also saw a rather large padlock hanging in the two big rings on both ends of the chain, which I was sure that the key that Dad had given me earlier would fit that very same lock.

Dad then warned me by saying, "The chain is a heavy-duty one and should be run around something like a pole or tree then back around the bike so that it will be there when you came back for it. Please try to remember what happened to your last bike, son."

I did not even wait to go any further to check out the bike, I just turned and hugged both my parents saying, "Thanks Mom and Dad, thanks a lot, you have made this the very best birthday ever!" I turned and hugged my little brother Rocky. He just looked up at me and said, "I love you and Happy Birthday Mickey!" I reached down and gave him another squeeze.

I walked back to survey my new bike. My heart seemed to be beating a million miles an hour. At this time, I thought, "I am so lucky to have parents that love me so very much." I could hardly wait to tell Tommy and Billy about my new bike. Then I noticed that this was not just an ordinary trail bike but instead was a top-of-the-line trail bike. I had only heard about them but had never seen one like it before now; it is a twenty-six-speed trail bike. I had heard they were very, very light. I picked it up, and, just as advertised, I was indeed able to pick it up using only one hand. As I lifted it, I did marvel at just how beautiful and light it was.

I then saw the brand name logo on the front fork of the bike, and I found it read, MUSTANG TWO. I suddenly remembered the joking comment that I had made earlier at the table was indeed correct. I thought how the question about the key fitting a Mustang was awesomely accurate. I laughed when I had said to Dad, "I always wanted a new Mustang." After a good laugh, I turned and walked back over to where Mom and Dad were standing. I gave both of them another hug and thanked them both by telling them, "Thanks again, Mom and Dad, for the greatest birthday ever. You have made me the happiest guy in the whole wide world. I can hardly wait to tell Tommy and Billy about the bike and of just how lucky I am."

We all filed back into the kitchen, while I was talking a mile a minute. I realized again just how very happy I was at that moment.

DISASTER STRIKES

As we got back to the kitchen, Dad asked both Rocky and me to please sit down at the table. As we both sat down, Mom moved close to Dad, and he put his arm around her shoulders. They stood just looking at each other for a few moments before talking.

He then began by stating, "We need to talk to you both before you go to school today. Your mother will be at school today, and she will be there to fill out the paperwork to take you both out of school." He paused again, as if to let his statement sink in. I looked back and forth between Mom and Dad, trying to grasp Dad's words, but his statement only brought about a flood of questions.

I regrouped my thoughts, and then I thought his statement had to be a big birthday joke. But that thought was shattered when he continued with, "We have to move." It was the look on my mom's face that let me know his statement was true. I could see tears welling up in my mom's eyes. I now know this whole thing is real, and something terrible is about to happen. I saw that it was now approaching seriously severe. A fear of the unknown sent a cold shiver down my backbone. I can never remember having this instant feeling of dread before in my life. I thought this couldn't be happening to me on the happiest day of my life. I loved it here, and all my friends were here.

I did not want to sound like I was rebellious, but to say I was upset would be an understatement. I have always been respectful towards my parents. So I tried to choose my words carefully because I felt the need to get that frustration out, or I thought I would burst.

I started to vent my feelings by saying, "But Dad, I don't want to go! All my friends live here! How can you and Mom do this to me?" I looked down at Rocky, and I could see the tears forming in his eyes as well.

It was then that I looked into my parent's eyes, and I could see that this was bothering them too. I knew that the way that I was feeling was very selfish on my part, but it hurt so much to even think of moving. I did not want to be rude to my parents, but I thought this impending move was going to be the end of the world for me! My life was going to be over, and this was just my twelfth birthday.

Dad, after the long pause, went on to tell us why. He then said, "Rocky and Mickey, I feel the need to explain why we have to move. The company I work for has given me no choice because they are relocating the entire company from Trenton, NJ to Vancouver, WA. They are shutting down the plant here and moving it to Vancouver. I am to take over the management of the new plant there. The company is transferring all the corporate offices there as well. So you see kids, I do not want to go out and find another job that will undoubtedly pay me much less than what I will be making when we do move."

He paused as if to let this all sink in.

After sitting there for a while, I asked, "When do we have to leave?"

My father paused again, then said, "I have to leave later this morning to catch a flight so that I can meet with the realtor in Vancouver; he has been looking for a new place just out of the city of Vancouver. I want it to be somewhat like it is here; your mother and I do not want to live right in the city." He went on, "The company is going to buy our house here, and then buy a bigger and better home for us over there, of our choosing. The buying us a new home is to compensate us for the move. They will also help us further by paying for the move, and there will be a very nice raise in salary as well."

He then went on, "I know it is going to be hard on both of you, but I ask you both to please help us get this done with the least amount of stress as possible."

Then my mom showed support for Dad by saying, "Kids, you will make new friends over there, and you'll both see once we get there that it will work out."

"But Dad, I don't want to move either," Rocky said.

Dad stated firmly, "I know, son, none of us want to do this. But guys, we do have to move, so I ask you both to try and make the best we can of this move."

It was at this time that I knew that there was no need to talk any more. My parents had their minds made up, and nothing was going to change their plans. I thought I would spite them and just quit doing my schoolwork when we get to our new home. I knew that would be the one big thing that would upset them the most, because I knew how important my grades are to them. I will make them pay for moving us across the country. Yes, I have made up my mind to become the human slug at this new school. I will stop playing football at this new school as well.

At the same time of being angry, I feel that down deep that my mom and dad were moving us only because they were trying to help the family. That thought brought about a feeling of guilt for my feelings of frustration of the impending move. I could only keep my fingers crossed that someway there would be a miracle, and we would not have to move.

When I got on the school bus, I began to cry, and the crying only made me even madder. I just hoped that no one would see my tears. I looked around and saw that no one seem to notice.

I centered my thoughts on my best friends, Tommy and Billy. I couldn't wait to tell them because just maybe they could come up with the idea that would save the day and cause us not to have to move. I couldn't let myself think that there was no hope at all on being able to turn this thing around so that this move would not need to happen.

When my school bus stopped at school, I jumped off the bus, and there was Tommy as always waiting for me. I told him the bad news as we walked, and his response was, "You can't move! We are a team, Billy, you and I are the Three Musketeers! We've always had plans to go to Harvard together and play football like your dad!"

I could see him fighting back his tears as we both turned to walk over to where Billy's bus usually arrived and waited for it. Soon, it came to a halt in front of us. Then Billy finally came out. I repeated to Billy all that I had told Tommy just a few moments before. I found that it was a little easier this time, but it still hurt like heck to say it. I told him, "My parents told Rocky and me this morning that we have to move right away. And we're leaving as soon as I get home. I explained to him the problem hoping that he might have an idea to stop this move.

I could tell by their actions that Tommy and Billy were both just as shocked as Rocky and I had been earlier this morning. Billy echoed Tommy's idea to a T, saying, "We always wanted to play football together in high school and college. Our plans have always been that you were to be the quarterback while Billy and I were going to be your receivers," and then he asks me, "Are your mom and dad going to take all that away from us?" But even as he spoke those words, I knew down deep just how selfish he sounded. When I realized it had been almost my exact feelings earlier this morning. A little guilt set in as I now fully realized what a selfish son I was being, but I wanted someone to please take away the pain.

I then felt that it was time that I felt a need to come to my parent's defense. I said, "He told us that it was vital because he would lose his job if we did not move."

They both said in unison, "It just isn't fair because we have all these plans." I couldn't agree with them more.

Yet at the same time, I found that same sinking feeling returning that I had felt earlier when Dad had told us that we had to move, only it was even bordering on panic now. I now felt that my life was over and that it will never be the same again. I might as well curl up and die. Maybe then they would be sorry for doing this to Rocky and me. Then I reflected on my thoughts of a truce earlier. Boy, was I ever feeling mixed up right now! My thoughts and feelings were going first one way then the other.

Then as if an afterthought, Tommy asked, "This is a joke, right?" I told him, "I wish it were, but it is no joke, my friend."

They both had this stunned look on their faces, as they both appeared to be just as defeated as I felt. We stood there for a few moments and said very little as if we were all three in a daze.

We finally walked into the school, and there at the front desk at the office was my mother. I knew the reason she was here was to check me out of school. My two buddies and I stopped for a few moments. When Mom looked up and saw us standing in the hallway, she just gave us a slight wave. I gave her a small wave back, and all three of us walked on to our classroom to start our last day of school together.

My thoughts were not on school today, but they were on the fear of moving and the need to have to make new friends. But I knew that I would never be able to find buddies like Tommy and Billy. I caught both of them watching me off and on all day, and I knew their thoughts were probably running along the same lines as mine.

School went by very slowly, or at least it seemed that way to me. When the day was over, I couldn't remember a single thing that was taught to me that day. It was a total loss, and no matter how hard I tried, I hadn't been able to come up with a plan to keep us from having to move. When the school bus was almost to our driveway, I suddenly realized I hadn't even told my buddies about my new bike. I made a mental note to call them later to let them know about my birthday present. I thought, "a lot of good that it would do now." I got off my bus and walked up the driveway; I felt the pain sweep back over me.

It was only then that I noticed an envelope sticking out of my backpack. I opened it, and there was a birthday card from Tommy and Billy. It had been made out and signed by both of them. But on the backside of the envelope as if it was an afterthought it said, "We don't want you to go, that is for sure, but if you do have to leave then just remember you'll always be our best friend, and it was signed, "Friends for life, Tommy and Billy." I held the card close to my chest and had a long, long cry. I found that as I cried, the thought of crying caused my frustration and anger to surged back with a vengeance. I kept thinking, "Why did this have to happen to me? Especially on my birthday, that had started as the happiest day of my life?"

CHAPTER THREE

THE NEW BEGINNING!

I said very little as Mom drove us across the country to Vancouver, WA, but I perked up when Mom finally said, "We're here!" As the car came to a halt, I bailed out and stood looking at our new house. I had to say it was pretty neat, it was unique in design, and I found the color blue was smart. I could see that it had been newly remodeled, but anyone could see that whoever had lived here had taken excellent care of it.

I quickly reflected on my commitment to make them pay.

Dad came up behind me and said, "Guys, all this is our new home and as far as you can see over to that fence line over there," pointing to a fence on our left, which looked like it was at least the length of two football fields away. Then he directed our attention by pointing to the right side of our yard, and I saw the fence line there. It appeared to be a little farther than three football fields away. Next, he turned our attention to the back boundary line and pointed to trees standing down over the small hill and stated, "That stand of trees way down there forms the back edge of our property line." He then went on, "And just on the other side of those trees is your new school." I noted the red rooftop that was barely visible through the treetops.

I could see a pathway that ran between the house and the garage then down over the small rise. As I looked at where the path went, I saw that it ran by an old oak tree that looked huge at this distance.

Dad then led Mom, Rocky, and me into the house. We entered into the back porch, which led to a second door, and when we passed through that door, we were in the kitchen. The kitchen was indeed a big one in comparison to our old kitchen. The size of this kitchen made it so that a person wanting to cook would have plenty of room to work without feeling cramped. There was a breakfast nook that was to one side of the kitchen, and I figured we would eat most of our meals there.

From the kitchen, Dad took us through a big archway that led into a rather large dining room about twenty feet square, and it had a large china hutch built into the wall for my mom's guest dishes and other knick-knacks. The big oak table that we had brought from the old house now sat in the middle of the new dining room, and I had to admit that it looked small sitting there.

We were then lead through another archway that led into the living room. The thing that drew my eye was the vast size of the massive fireplace with a large mantel. The room overall looked to be at least thirty feet long and over twenty feet wide. Running along the outside wall of the room was the most significant picture window that I had ever seen. It surveyed our whole backyard. I could see very clearly the big oak tree standing at the right edge of our yard. I had only glanced at it earlier upon our arrival here. I took a more extended look at the tree. I found that the added height gained from standing in the living room, I could get a much better look at just how massive that oak tree appeared.

I just stared for a few moments and was awestruck with how beautiful that the scene looked. In my mind, I noted it looked like a big oil painting rather than a big picture window. And the view reminded me of one time when Mom had taken Rocky and me to the museum, and we had seen a lot of oil paintings of scenery there. What I was seeing would have rivaled any of those paintings.

A shudder of guilt came to mind, from the feeling of enjoying even a minute was in some way, that I was disloyal to my friends back home. I once again renewed my vowed to make my mom and dad pay for moving me here.

The frustration with my feelings at this point is that I know down deep that my mom and dad had no choice in this move. When I am this upset, even when I knew they had no other option, it only fueled my guilt even more. I thought that I needed to give this more thought and somehow come to grips with all these mixed-up feelings as soon as possible.

I bounced back to the here and now as Mom took over the tour. She said, "Please follow us, boys," as Dad fell in behind Mom and Rockey, and I followed Dad as we all exited the living room.

And as we then walked down the hallway, I could see that when Mom took us to the first doorway and as she opened that door, she stated, "This room will be our study/library."

I looked at Dad's many law books already placed on the shelves. I further recognized that many books on the shelves had been stored in boxes in our old garage back home. We never had shelves in our old house that could hold all those books. I found all of them were now on these shelves here. I thought it looked like all of Dad's books were on the shelves too. Still, the abundant shelving here was not full at all, even with all those books on them, they had some room to spare.

Mom led us on down the hallway we found that the second door on the left was Mom and Dad's bedroom. I looked in, thinking of how big this room was. In their old bedroom, my mom's and dad's king-sized bed always seemed so big. But now, in this newer bigger bedroom, that same bed looked somewhat smaller. I also noticed that they had full-length sliding mirrors hung on each of the doors of their closet, making the bedroom even look more open. They had a white carpet on their floor. It was at this time that Mom said, "Boys, this is the last time that anyone will wear shoes in the house. We will do as they do in Japan and take our shoes off before coming into the main part of the house. We will then put them in the cabinet that you passed by on the back porch. By doing this, we feel it is the only way that we can keep all the carpets in the house looking good for a long, long time." I looked at Dad, and he was nodding his head yes in agreement with all she had said.

Mom now asked, "Boys, why not check out your things in your room?"

I turned and walked on down the hallway, found the next door on the right; I figured that that was going to be Rocky's and my room. As I entered, the very first thing I saw was that the boxes stacked in the middle of the room all had Rocky's name on them, and for a second, I was puzzled, where was my stuff? Then I ask myself, could it be true? Mom and Dad hadn't said anything about our room arrangements. I couldn't believe that I might have a bedroom of my own. I looked back at my father and mother, who both had a smile on their lips. Then Dad answered my unspoken question by saying, "Why don't you have a look at your room Mickey?"

As I entered the hallway again, I saw the last door on the left, and as I opened it, I viewed the most fabulous sight to me as I saw all my stuff in the middle of the room. Dad had made my bed, and I took notice that he had hung my curtains that had all the NFL teams' logos on them.

I found that this room was a tad bit bigger than Rocky's. Like Rocky's room, my things had placed mine in the middle of my bedroom as well. I moved over to where my boxes were stacked. I then stopped and slowly turned around, checking out the whole room and found that I was looking at the most beautiful bedroom in the whole wide world. I had a tough time not letting out a big war-whoop and giving away my happiness with our new bedroom arrangements because I was so very, very happy right now.

In the old house, Rocky and I had always slept in the same room with me. Even though I loved him dearly, there were moments when we had our arguments and disagreements over him getting into my things. Mom tried putting tape down the middle of our room to keep us separated, but that had only worked for a short time. Then as if Rocky couldn't handle it anymore, he came to get on my side of the room and right into my things. Getting into my stuff was not the worst of it; the worst was Rocky broke many of my belongings while looking at them that bothered me most. I got frustrated, then Rocky would look up at me to tell me he was sorry, it would soften my heart, and I forgave him again and again. Now I hoped that just maybe "out of sight, out of mind" would rule the day!

When I looked up, I saw Mom and Dad standing in the doorway, looking at me. I did not want them to know just how much I liked this place we were to now call home. I found though I was having a harder and harder time staying mad. Then Dad asked, "How do you like the place so far?" I just shrugged my shoulders, not wanting him to know how I felt, saying, "It's OK, I guess." I could see the look in both my parent's eyes and knew that I had hurt them both with my indifferent answer. This hurtful manner brought about a very, very bad feeling in my heart. I knew down deep that we had to move. Now, I felt the fight leaving me of wanting to get even for moving all of us here. And at that second, I felt sad, because if I were to like it here, then I would become a traitor to my best buddies back home. The pain that I was causing my mom and dad right then made me feel very, very sad inside; I felt torn between the loyalty of my parents, whom I love dearly against that of my commitment to my good friends back home. This war was eating at me.

I turned my head so they could not see the tears that were beginning to form in the corners of my eyes. I quickly wiped my eyes, and when I looked back around, I found that Mom and Dad had already turned and walked back down the hallway towards the kitchen.

I stopped to see how Rocky was doing. There was a smile on his face that made me feel even a little guiltier. Because I could see just how happy he was to have his room as I was with mine.

CHAPTER FOUR

NEW FRIENDS

As I reentered the kitchen, Dad said, "Why don't we all take a walk after we finish lunch? We can all see your new school." I asked, "Will we be walking to school rather than ride the bus?" Dad answered, "Yes." Rocky chimed in with, "Walk to school? I can't walk that far, Dad!" Dad chuckled and said, "You don't even know how far it is Rocky, so let's take that walk after lunch, and then we'll see just how far away it is!"

We gobbled down lunch, then got up to take our walk. As we walked out of the house and turned toward the back yard, I marveled once again at the huge back yard. My first thought was, "do we get a riding lawnmower?" I made a mental note to cover that with my dad later as the mowing of the yard back home had always been my job. All four of us walked between the house and the big three-car garage. I looked at the garage and quietly wondered if my new bike was in there.

I noticed the well-worn pathway I had seen earlier. We stopped several times while Dad pointed out things he thought were important. I was still surprised when he told us again that the land we were walking on was all ours.

We crested the hill, and while looking back to our right, I saw that there was a rather large creek that started way back somewhere to our right, and I traced the flow as it turned and started to run parallel to our pathway. I saw that the creek ran down the gentle slope of the land. Then the stream disappeared out in front of us. My interest perked up even more when I saw nice-sized trout swim away from us as we skirted the creek. As we walked on down the pathway, I could see down the hill. From this distance, now I could see more of the big oak tree and marveled at its truly colossal size. I realized that the picture I had seen looking out the picture window did not do this big tree justice. The massive tree was right in the middle of the pathway! As we got closer, I could see that the well-worn path split around the tree on both sides. Dad confirmed that the tree was indeed an oak tree. I rubbed my hand on the mighty oak tree as we went around it.

I thought about having a fishing hole right in my back yard. If only I had my buddies here to go fishing with, it would be perfect. This thought made me sad again.

We walked only a few hundred feet more down the hill. I could make out just a little more of our new school through the trees. We went a few hundred feet further, and when we broke out into an opening, there was the school just to our left.

We had crossed over a footbridge that went over the creek. It ran along the edge of the path, then turned left and ran along the side of the school football field and playgrounds.

Down deep, I was glad that we lived so close to the school. I was looking forward to that walk to school each day as a chance to clear my mind before classes started.

But then I reflected on my commitment not to play football again to get back at my mom and dad for making me move here. Then I decided to change my mind because punishing them would only hurt me. So I will play football here, but I just won't be doing schoolwork. That will bug my parents the most anyway.

I took notice that there were five guys playing football out on the field. My heart raced just a little at the thought of playing football almost in my back yard. There were also a couple of other boys playing one-on-one basketball in the paved fenced-in part of the playground. I could make out another large group of kids that were playing inside the chain-link fence that ran along the pathway leading towards the school.

But it was the guys that were playing football that piqued my interest the most. I thought just maybe this would not be a total loss after all. We played at our school back home, but the field was about three miles from my old place. I stopped for a second to watch with more focus on those five playing in the game. After all, it is my first love in and of all sports. The boys were really into their game, and it appeared that they had not even noticed my family and me.

I turned and walked to catch up with my mom and dad to take a look at the rest of the school. But I was brought up short when one of the boys called out, "Hey, are you the new kid?" I turned around to see if he was talking to me. Sure enough, he was looking right at me. I nodded my head, yes. The one that had spoken came toward us holding the football under his arm. The other four boys came trotting over to where we stood. I had taken a couple of steps towards them at the same time. As we got closer, I saw his hand come up for a handshake. I took his hand firmly as I returned his handshake, and he said his name was Biff. Then the rest had come up and stood behind the guy. Biff turned towards the other four and introduced each one. My thought was that I hoped I would remember their names the next day. As he introduced me to the rest, they all shook my hand as well. One of the kids' names was the same as one of my friends back home, Tommy.

Then I turned and introduced my mom, my dad, and my little brother to them.

Biff then asks, "Do you like to play football?" I nodded my head, yes. He asks, "What position do you like to play?" I told him, "In my other school, I played quarterback."

He nodded his head yes and said, "That's fantastic we'll set the teams if you want to play, I can be the quarterback on one team, and you can be the one for the other team. We'll have equal teams that way. Can you play now, Mickey?" he asked. I looked at Mom and Dad. They both nodded yes. I found myself very, very happy. Dad said, "Please remember our rule that you are to be home before dark, son."

I had a great time with my new friends and thought how glad I was that I changed my mind about not playing football.

As I entered the back door, I saw the sign that I recognized as Dad's handwriting. It was outside the back door where we would enter the kitchen through the back porch. The sign said, "PLEASE REMEMBER TO REMOVE YOUR SHOES BEFORE ENTERING!" I did as the sign said and sat on the stool and took off my shoes. I opened the cabinet that was nearby; there were shelves inside divided into cubbies labeled with names. I found my name and took my slippers out and placed my street shoes in their place. I found Mom's, Dad's, and Rocky's footwear were all in each of their cubbies.

I could smell the food even before I opened the door from the back porch, and realized I was starving. I ran in and washed my hands. We sat down at the table, and Dad led us as always in saying the grace over the food. I also noticed as I had walked through the kitchen that Mom had most of her kitchen already organized, and I had to admit that it was looking great.

We chatted at the table as we ate, and Mom and Dad both took turns asking me about my afternoon. They asked me about my new friends, and how the game went. I told them that my team didn't win, but it had been by a small margin. I also said that I was sure that as we all got to know each other better than the scores would be even closer.

At the end of the dinner, Dad handed Rocky and me our chore lists for the new house. Rocky and I both read them. I noticed that there were a few less chores for me than I had had at our old home. Dad told Rocky the reason for the change was because Rocky was older, and now he had to share more of the family chores. When I heard that news, it made me even happier. But then again, I didn't want them to know that just yet.

CHAPTER FIVE

NEW SCHOOL

I had the first day jitters. As we walked along, Rocky was chattering away, telling me about some of the kids he met yesterday. He went on talking about how much he liked the new school and all its new playground equipment and how great his new friends were. I listened to him talk and realized just how happy he had become.

I thought that the concerns that were bugging me more than likely went through every new kid's mind that moved into a new school.

Will the kids here like me?

Will I fit in here?

Will the kids here want me to be their friend?

I found as I listened to Rocky, I felt better about our move here. I then thought to myself that I no longer felt apprehensive about some of the questions that I had before moving here.

I knew five of the kids at this school already, because I had met them and had played football with them. The question that I had now was would they act today as they had yesterday when we played football. Or would the five guys pretend they didn't even know me today when they got around all their friends? Being the new kid in school was all new to me as I had never been the new kid before now. I was so glad when I entered the school grounds, and I saw them coming out to meet me. I found that my new friends from yesterday gave me the impression by the way that they were coming to meet me that they were glad to see me. Their actions did give me a feeling of relief that they were happy to see me and made me feel very welcome here. As we got closer together, I could see a big smile on Biff's face, and it looked to me as if he had an important idea that no one knew but him.

Biff said, "There's someone I need for you to meet. Because she told me she would beat on me if I didn't introduce the two of you first thing today." This statement made me feel outstanding, and Biff chuckled.

My thoughts surged, to think that anyone in a new school would want to meet me? This statement of wanting to meet me made me feel super. But then I thought Biff said "she," didn't he? I have stated earlier just what I think about girls. After all, they can't even play football, now can they?

We walked over toward a rather large group of girls. We stopped just short of the group, and Biff motioned to someone in the group. I tried to see who he was waving to, but I couldn't tell until she stepped out of the group and came toward us.

I never had a girlfriend, and it made me a little nervous to think that a girl in this new school would even know about me, let alone want to know me. It was not an unfamiliar experience for me as other girls had tried to become my girlfriend back home. I had never taken any of them up on the offer to be my girlfriend, because I never felt I had time for a girlfriend. I had my sports, and then there was homework and fishing, and so I never thought that I had the time left over for a girlfriend.

I can say, though, that it did feel good that anyone from this new school would want to know me.

As I was looking at the girl in front of us, I noticed how pretty she was. Her long blond hair kind of matched mine, and then as she got closer, it was her smile and her eyes that were so outstanding.

Biff looked at her then at me and said, "Mickey, this is my little sister Becky. She saw you yesterday when we were playing football, and she told me that she wanted to meet you."

Becky did not appear to be the least bit nervous or uneasy about our meeting. I stuck out my hand, and she took my hand in hers. As I shook her hand, I said, "Pleased to meet you, Becky." I noticed she was blushing, but, even though a little embarrassed, she didn't waver when she said, "I am so glad to meet you, Mickey." As I looked deep into her eyes, there was a feeling that came over me that I had never felt before. The best way for me to describe what I was feeling was like a warm nervous flutter in the pit of my stomach. I extended my hand for a handshake. As she took my right hand, I noticed that my hand was sweaty. She was holding her books close to her chest with her left hand. As we shook hands, I realized for the first time in my life that I did not want to turn this girl's hand loose. I knew that it was well beyond time for us to release the handshake, but I just wanted to look into her light blue eyes. I couldn't look away from them, and she seemed to be feeling the same as I was. It would appear she, too, did not appear to be in any rush to release my hand either.

It was Biff's voice that finally brought us both back to the here and now when he said, "I hope you two will get to know each other better." As we pulled out hands apart, she was looking up into my eyes kind of funny. The look in her eyes made me feel terrific, and that fluttering feeling was getting even more energetic.

Becky looked away from my eyes and dropped her chin down a little. Then she looked back up at me with those beautiful blue eyes and a very coy expression, and I knew that I wanted more than anything to be near this girl.

When I did tear my eyes from hers and looked back into Biff's eyes, I saw that they were the same color.

Then there was a momentary thought that I was too young to be feeling this way about any girl. I thought that this was something way out of my ability to turn off. This girl, Becky, had in a matter of minutes, made me feel so great. I also knew right then and there that I wanted her to be my girlfriend.

I asked her, "Can I see you at the lunch period?"

She blushed a little more but answered right up, "Yes, I would love to eat lunch with you, Mickey." A feeling of pride went through me because she had said yes. All I could do was look at her and felt my neck and face starting to get very hot. She was so cute; I knew that I was blushing, but for some reason, I didn't care.

All I could say, "Thanks, Becky!"

I looked back at Biff, and he had this kind of smirk look on his face as if he knew a secret as his knowing smile spread into a bigger smile. I turned away from Becky to follow Biff, and she turned to reenter her group of girlfriends.

I looked back over my shoulder and said just loud enough to be sure she could hear me saying, "See you at lunch then." She nodded yes and turned and continued to walk back to other girls. The girls began to chatter amongst themselves as we walked away.

Biff and I continued walking back to the rest of the boys. He and the other guys took me all around the school. They showed me our classroom last. I found out then that all six of us were in the same classroom. I also found out that Biff was the class president.

Everywhere we went, he would introduce me as, "This is my new friend Mickey." His introduction made me feel very, very good. Biff handled himself with confidence at all times. I felt so lucky that we had met the day before. This previous meeting had made it so much easier for me today.

As we walked around the hallways, I found myself looking for Becky. I was disappointed at not being able to find her.

I also learned that we were not going to be transferring to different classrooms for each subject that we took. We would be in the same classroom all day except for two classes, which would be P.E., and the other would be music. In my old school we would go to a different classroom and a different teacher for each subject.

As we entered the classroom, I found that every seat was full, except for two in the middle of the room.

I was pleasantly surprised to find that Becky was also in our classroom. Thinking back to what was said, when Biff introduced us, "This is my little sister." I then realized that he had made a play on words, but the question still stood there to be answered. So I leaned over and asked Biff, "I thought you said that she was your younger sister?" He laughed and said, "Mickey, we're twins, and it's a joke between us because I was born first by a little over two minutes. And that my friend is why I can honestly say, I am the oldest, and she is indeed my little sister." He continued with, "Our whole family is very close, but Becky and I are even closer." He looked at me and said, "I would be upset if she were to get hurt by anyone in any way!" I assumed he meant this as a warning, and I took it as just that. I wasn't offended by his statement. I felt the same way about my young brother Rocky. I also knew he meant what he said. I had no intention of hurting Becky.

As we walked into the front of the classroom, our teacher was standing there. Biff said, "Mr. Blinker, I would like to introduce you to Mickey Hunter." Then Biff turned and sat in his seat.

Mr. Blinker turned to me and said, "You must be the new student the office said I could expect today. I'm glad to meet you." He picked up a piece of paper from his desk handed it to me and said, "Mickey, I don't have a long list of rules in my classroom, but the ones I have I enforce. Please read these rules, sign at the bottom, and have your parents sign there too. Then please turn it back into me tomorrow." I nodded and shook his outstretched hand. I said, "Mr. Blinker, I'm glad to make your acquaintance." He looked at me and said, "Well done, Mickey!"

He turned to the class and said, "I do hope that each one of you will make Mickey feel welcome in our school."

I thought that it was funny when most of the class turned and looked at Becky. She just blushed and dropped her head.

Mr. Blinker assigned a seat to me, and I sat down. It was one of the two desks that had been unoccupied in the middle of the classroom. I discovered that Biff was right across the aisle from me.

Not meaning to, but I found that I was spending a lot of time turning around to watch Becky. I also found that the funny feeling that I had had earlier was now growing even more powerful. I hardly heard very much the teacher had to say that morning. I kept looking at the clock, thinking about lunch with Becky.

Finally, the bell rang, and it was lunchtime. I felt torn between going with Biff and the guys and wanting to be with Becky. Becky won out.

I waited for her in the front of the classroom. We strolled and chatted, asking and answering questions as we walked down to the cafeteria. I found that I was in no hurry. She seemed to be in no rush to get there either, and as we talked, I hung on her every word.

I was shocked when she reached up and took my hand. It felt good holding her hand, and she was the one who grabbed my hand. At first, holding hands made me feel kind of funny. That feeling passed after only a few steps. After a few more steps, the concern faded, and then it was gone. Holding hands with Becky now felt perfectly natural as we interlaced our fingers. But the funny fluttery feeling I was feeling again was now as if it were a million butterflies trying to get out of my stomach all at the same time. I have never felt this way in my whole life.

We worked our way through the lunch line. We then found a table towards the back of the lunchroom, and as we placed our food tray down, we sat down at a table side by side. We began to talk again, and I also found it ultimately comfortable to chat with her. I took stock in the way she looked, and that funny feeling at the pit of my stomach seemed to grow even stronger.

She wanted to know if I had a girlfriend back where I used to live. I told her, "I have a lot of friends, and several of them were girls." but added quickly, "but no real girlfriends."

She smiled and said, "Mickey, I saw you yesterday when you and my brother were playing football with Biff and his friends. When Biff and I got home, I made him promise to introduce us today."

I told her, "I didn't see where you were yesterday."

She said, "Some of the girls and I were practicing cheers on the other side of the school. When we took a break to get a drink, and it was then that I saw you and the other boys playing football. As I watched you guys play, I saw you were a very, very good player." She continued, "The longer I watched, I found that I liked you right away."

I know that I must have been blushing because my face was boiling. I did not know what to say. After a brief moment that seemed like forever, I finally said, "I do wish I had seen you too. It would have made me want to get to school this morning so much easier." She laughed and looked away, and when she turned back, she was just smiling. She looked down, then looked up again with that coy look, and my stomach fluttered once again. We just sat in silence for several moments. It was the bell ringing that brought me to my senses. That bell ringing almost made me mad because I didn't want to go back to class. I wanted to just sit here with her until school was out. When we rose to dump our trays, I noticed that neither of us had eaten very much of our lunch. I looked down at them and said, "Looks like we wasted this meal."

Becky said, "I want to get to know you, Mickey. I can't remember a meal that I have enjoyed so much in my whole life."

Without saying another word, she just reached over and kissed me on the cheek. It happened so fast that it caught me off guard. But I found that kiss on the cheek made me want to kiss her back, but I did not follow through with that want.

We entered the classroom just before the tardy bell rang. I could feel that almost all the students were watching us as we sat down. Biff looked at me and mouthed great going and gave me a thumbs up. I just smiled back.

During class, even when I was looking at the teacher, it was Becky's face that kept coming into my mind. I didn't hear much of what was said in the afternoon classes, even though they were my two favorites. They were science and math, but I was just not into them today.

As I reviewed the day in my mind, I realized I couldn't get Becky off my mind since I met her this morning. I found that no matter how hard I tried to focus my thoughts on school or other things, she was right in the middle of those thoughts again. But then, on the other hand, after really thinking about it, I did not want that feeling to fade either.

A question quickly crossed my mind, "Was this what my dad felt when he had met my mom for the first time?"

We had planned to play football right after school. But for the first time in my life, my mind was not on football. I apologized to the guys and told them, "I can't play today because I have some things to work out in my mind. I'm sure I'll be alright tomorrow." With that, Biff walked with me to the edge of our property that ran up to my house.

We stopped and turned to face each other, and then Biff asked, "Is everything alright?"

I shrugged my shoulders and told him, "I don't know for sure, Biff, but I can tell you that sister of yours is very special to me." I went on to tell him, "I know, Biff, that on the one hand, I am too young to be thinking about girls the way I am right now. But on the other hand, I can honestly say the way I feel about Becky that I've never felt this way about any girl in my life. These feelings are completely foreign to me, Biff." I then concluded with, "I just need time alone to sort through these feelings, Biff."

He laughed and said, "Just maybe you're in love, Mickey?"

I was stunned. I had not even thought about that. I knew what love was because I loved my parents, and my little brother, and the love that my parents show for each other and to both Rocky and me. I do recognize that kind of love, but this is quite different.

I looked into my mind, and for the first time since I have met Becky this morning, I was asking myself, could this be like the love my parents feel for each other?

Biff just smiled and hit me playfully on the shoulder, saying, "I'll see you tomorrow morning, my friend!"

With that, we broke off and waved at each other. I walked up the pathway leading to the house. I was deep in thought as I walked.

I could just see the big oak tree standing in the middle of the pathway; I noticed something at the stream bank right under the tree.

The movement from whatever it was had caught my eye.

I could now see that at the very edge of the creek bank stood a raccoon. As I got closer, I could see she had three babies trailing along behind her. I stopped and watched with complete fascination. The mother's movements soon told me that she was teaching the three little ones to fish for crawdads. She did this by reaching her paws down into the water, and it appeared that she was using her one paw as a lure and by dangling it in the water and moving it slowly back and forth. Then a crawdad would reach up and grab hold of her paw; she would then grab the crawdad quickly with both hands trapping it. She would then take it out of the water before it could let go of her paw. She then bit the head, killing the crawdad. She then turned and gave the dead crawdad to one of her babies.

I found this to be fascinating. I had never seen a raccoon in the wild, so I had never seen one acting this way before. I watched her repeat this action until all three of her babies had a crawdad to eat. Then and only then did she stop fishing and took the last one she caught and began eating it herself? I was disappointed when she finally looked down the pathway towards me, and when she saw me, she stopped, and at this time, she then stood up on her hind legs as if to get a better look.

She made chattering sounds catching the three baby's attention. Her three babies stopped eating and followed her obediently across the creek. They quickly disappeared through the willows that bordered the creek bank on the other side.

I went to where I thought I had seen them disappear. I balanced on several large rocks that stuck out of the water crossing without getting my feet wet. I arrived at the other side of the creek, parted the willows, and when I peered through, I was more than a little surprised when I found that there was a hidden pond.

I then noted that this particular pond was on our property and decided right then that this pond would my secret hiding place.

I noted that there were no human tracks on the other side of the willows but plenty of animal tracks.

I looked up and saw the mother raccoon and her babies again. They were still fishing for crawdads at the edge of the water. The raccoons were working their way around to where the creek flowed into the pond. I also noticed that the little ones were starting to fish for crawdads by themselves. I thought how remarkable that they were able to pick up that skill so very quickly. I parted the willows trying to be as quiet as I could. I did not want to disturb them and frighten them away as I already had done.

I noticed as I walked through that there was a huge old tree that had fallen and formed part of a dam that was making the pond. I found after looking harder that beavers had made the rest of the dam and then took note of the beaver lodge out in the middle of the pond.

I quietly and slowly crept over the old log and sat in the warm, dry sand on the other side of the creek, and rested my back against the trunk of the big tree. I was watching two things. One was the raccoons at the edge of the pond still fishing, and second was to see if I could see any of the beavers that had built the dam.

It was so relaxing and warm sitting there. As I watched the mother and her babies, I found I was still fascinated by the actions of the four of them.

Because of the warm sunshine and the stress of the day, I relaxed, and soon I drifted off and found myself fast asleep.

CHAPTER SIX

A RUDE AWAKENING!

It was a big clap of thunder that shook the ground that woke me. I was so scared! And the thing that bothered me the most was that I could not remember for a few moments exactly where I was, or even how I had gotten here. There was a flash of lightning, and then another clap of thunder that shook the ground again. I was very stiff from sitting there so long. It still took me a few moments more to get my bearings. Then in a flash, I remembered just where I was and just how I had gotten there. I stood there getting my bearings, while bracing myself on to a log, I quickly got up and headed back the way I had come getting to the pond. Then I realized how very late it was.

I felt an inner panic start to build in me. I felt the need to get home, like an hour ago.

I quickly scrambled back over the rocks and noted again just how dark it was getting. There were many flashes of lightning right overhead, and the thunder rolled, shaking the ground every time it clapped so loud.

Then it hit me just how mad my mom and dad were going to be when I did get home. They had always told me that they expected me to be home before dark. I also remembered the chores that I had to do after school every day.

I hurriedly scrambled up the bank of the creek, and I was just barely able to see the pathway.

Fear jolted my thoughts once again to just how upset they were going to be with me. I knew the rules, and the one that was most important to them was about being out this close to dark without permission.

My mind started to play mental games to justify being so late. I thought that maybe I could skirt around the rule, as it wasn't quite dark yet. Yet my mind quickly put a kybosh on that idea knowing in my heart that it would not fly. I knew they would see through that ploy in a heartbeat.

I once again realized that it was getting darker by the minute, stirring within me an even a more significant need to hurry. With my feet still dry, I pushed faster as I tried to move my stiff body along while there was still enough daylight to make out the pathway.

I picked up my pace faster and faster with each flash of lightning and clap of thunder.

Once again, I looked up and took stock of just how dark it was getting to be.

There was another lightning flash, and it seemed that it was right overhead again, and for a moment, the lightning flash brightened up the whole sky, but only for a split second. But I found that the momentary brightness did not calm my fast-beating heart. The next flash did light up the big oak tree right in front of me.

Immediately the thunder clapped, and it seemed that it was even louder if that could be possible. Then the lighting seemed to snap in rapid succession. It sounded like there were three or four more claps, then the thunder rolled in quick succession right behind the flashes. It appeared that it was never going to stop, and this took my thoughts away from my dad's possible anger for a moment. I could feel my heart pounding like a sledgehammer, and as I got closer to the big oak tree, another flash of lightning made me see the tree clearly. As I closed in on the big tree, I placed my left hand on the bark, trying to grab the big tree to help me spin around it faster.

And that was all I remembered, reaching out to touch that tree, and then there was silence.

CHAPTER SEVEN

HERE COMES THE BIG DOG

The next thing that I became aware of was that I find that I was lying on my back. I felt something massive on top of me. The flashes of lightning helped me to see somewhat, but for some reason, I was having a hard time focusing my eyes. I could just make out a big massive furry thing on top of me. But my eyes that were not seeing things were fuzzy!

Because of its big size and heavyweight, I asked myself if this could be a bear. The next thing that began to seep through my brain was the smell of singed hair.

I ran my hands up the sides of this thing that was on top of me. The thought that I had was that it was a bear. The reason I thought that it was a bear was because of the weight of the animal. But then as my hands felt along, I felt something wet. I brought my fingers back to my nose to try and identify that it was indeed blood and burned fur. But that fear of a bear quickly left me. When flash of lightning lit up the area, and it showed me that it was indeed a very, very big dog, not a bear.

My thoughts raced a mile a minute, and I tried to filter out what had brought me to having this big black dog on top of me.

CHAPTER EIGHT

MY NEW FRIEND

My eyes were not focusing, and no matter how many times I blinked my eyes, they did not seem to want to clear. The fuzzy sight that I was having, along with the fear of being late, stepped in and raised its ugly head again. I ask myself, would I be partially blind now, and what the heck had happened?

Then as a few more minutes passed, and my mind and eyes started to clear somewhat, I realized that, yes, I would probably be all right. That thought came about because I found that my sight was slightly better now.

I breathed a sigh of relief because my eyesight was clearing reasonably fast now.

I then ran my hands down the animal's fur. I realized that it was dead weight, and I figured that the animal's weight was almost equal to mine.

Thoughts were bouncing around in my mind, but soon it centered on the question of what had just happened? No answer came to mind, and I then noticed that my ears were ringing not loud, but there was a challenging ringing in my ears nonetheless.

I rolled the big dog off of me, and, as I got up, I became painfully aware of my stiffness and the burning on each side of my chest. When I touched each side of the middle of my chest and ran my finger delicately over the burning place on both sides, I found it to be like the worst sunburn I can ever remember having. I withdrew my fingers and stopped rubbing the spots.

I noticed a dull pain in my head, and then it was gone.

But my recollection of what had happened was still quite fuzzy. I found that as I was rubbing my eyes, it seemed to help some, and now my thoughts were getting more precise.

I now looked with a clearing eye and could see the big black dog lying on the pathway. My eyesight was much better but still not entirely focused, and that fact made me mad to think that I needed to see, and it was taking my body so long to get it straight.

With the limited light, I could just barely see the dog. I could only see the dark-furred dog because the path was a lighter color.

As I bent down to stroke the big dog, and I felt something that went through me like a mild electric shock. It did not hurt, but as it entered my body, I felt a super surge of something like electricity again but much softer this time.

The second surge brought a super-strong connection with this big dog. I can say with assurance that I have never felt this way for any other animal before.

It's not like I didn't like dogs; I just never made this type of caring connection with one before.

I felt a strong need to get this dog to help. It also seemed that this was an emergency.

I could feel that he was still breathing. I thought that I needed to get help as fast as I could because I believed that this big dog was in danger of losing his life.

I knew that there was not any way I could ever in a million years move this big dog on my own. I would need to go and get my dad to help me.

My eyes were almost entirely back to normal. I knew that I could see well enough to stay on the pathway, and I felt my strength beginning to return.

I could feel that the need for help was the top priority for me right now.

I realized this strong feeling that I felt about the dog I would never be able to explain this feeling to anyone in a million years.

I could see it much better now, and I noticed that the dog was still not awake. But I could feel the dog breathing, and this brought a feeling of relief. I felt calmer now.

It seemed that with this calmer feeling covered me like a big cloak, and, with this new feeling, I found an uncontrollable need to touch this big dogs head.

I reached down and placed both of my hands on the top of the dogs head. Almost at once, when I touched his head, I felt something like a soft tingle of an electric charge, and it caused the palms of my hands to tingle. This feeling passed through my hands and then through all my fingers and then back into the dog's head.

As I left the dog and hurried up the path, I noticed that my sight was now back to normal. It happened very fast, and I also noticed that the ringing in my ears was all gone as well. I breathed a sigh of relief as I hurried up the pathway towards home. I stopped only once to look back, but the darkness prevented me from seeing anything. I knew that it would be complete darkness in a few minutes.

I hurried on up the path, and now I could see the lights glowing from my new home. Seeing the lights made me feel better, but it was the silhouette of a man that brought concern to my heart.

I knew that it was my father's outline. I could see that from the way he was standing with his arms crossed and legs spread for balance just how upset he was.

That first fear that I had when I awoke from the thunder was back, like unto a warning that was about to come true. I was in deep, deep trouble, and for once, I could honestly say I did not know what had happened to me. But I felt that concern was about to overtake and crush me, and it was almost overwhelmed me.

I saw my dad uncross his arms as I approached and with his hands clenched into fists as they now rested on each hip. The first words I heard were, "Where have you been, young man?" And even before I could answer, he asks briskly another question, "Do you know how worried that your mom and I have been? Son, I have been back and forth to the school three times searching for you. Your mother and I have been worried sick about you, Mickey. We thought that something terrible had happened to you."

With that and even before I could answer again, he grabbed me and gave one of the biggest hugs I ever had from him. His voice cracked as he said, "Son, I could only imagine what could have happened to you. You cannot even think of all the things that ran through my mind. Please do not scare us like this ever again."

I looked up into his eyes and said, "I am so very, very sorry, Dad, but I fell asleep coming home from school."

I felt the need to talk fast to let him know what had happened and give me the help I needed with the big dog. I felt that time was of the essential, and the need for support for the big dog was right now.

To me right now, the big dog's need for help, overrode any fear of the trouble that loomed in front of me.

I said very quickly, "Dad, I know that I have not been at my best lately, and I promise to try and do better. But, right now, I need your help! I need you to give me a hand to help a dog that is hurt quite badly!"

Dad stopped and stared at me for a moment then asked, "What dog, we don't have a dog, and we don't have any plans to have one!"

I said, "Yes, I know Dad, but he is hurt! And when I woke up, he was on top of me. I don't know what happened, I had fallen asleep, and when I woke up there he was on top of me, please help me, Dad, please!"

Dad stuttered, "What *on top of you*, did he hurt you?"

Even in the dim light filtering upon us from the house, I could see the concern in his eyes as he waited for my answer.

I went on repeating my request, "Dad, just please help me, he is hurt bad, and he needs our help right now! Please, Dad! I will explain the best I can later. Please trust me, Dad, and please help me to be able to help him, please!"

He then paused, looking down at me and then said, "If we are to do this, then there is something that you must do first, and that is to let your mother know that you are alright. When I couldn't find you anywhere, she like me has been so very, very worried about you, son!"

He paused, holding me by the shoulders at arm's length looked at me for what seemed like for a long time.

Then without saying anything else, he just gave me another big hug, and as he did so, he then turned and yelled over his shoulder. "Honey, why don't you come and see what the cat's drug in." In the same breath, he said, "And please clear off the kitchen table and put a clean sheet over it. We are going to bring in a dog that was hurt; it is one that Mickey is trying to save."

I chuckled to myself when I took a second to think about the fact that my mother was able to move that fast. When she came busting out the back door, her speed reminded me of an NFL linebacker busting through a line. Then swooping down, and in one motion, she had picked me up in her arms. She hugged me so hard; her grip was so tight I had a hard time breathing. As she hugged me, she began to cry. I saw tears streaking down her face as the light from the house reflected off her tears. She quickly asked, "Are you truly alright?"

I didn't want to slow things down, so I just nodded yes. The fact was that statement was not a lie because now my hearing and eyesight were back to normal. The only thing wrong with me now was the burn on my chest, and I didn't want to slow things down by trying to tell Mom about something I couldn't explain in a million years. I knew in my mind that it would be much better to try and sort that out later.

The fear for the dog reentered my brain once again. I didn't want to delay my return to the dog.

So I remained somewhat patient, knowing down deep that this would be the fastest means the rescue of my dog.

So with that thought in mind, I let her survey me over, so she would then be convinced that all was well.

I could feel the tension of the moment lift a little bit as she gave me another big hug as if to reassure herself that I was in one piece with no body parts missing.

That hug felt good, and it let me know that both of my parents loved me.

I knew that my being back home unharmed was what was most important to them both. Then my mom held me out to arm's length by my shoulders. As she then looked deep into my eyes once again. It was as if Mom was acting on an old proverb that said that the eye is the window into one's soul. With this reassurance clearly in her mind, she then released her grip and stated firmly, "You had us all so anxious, even Rocky was crying for you."

With that, Rocky came bursting out from behind Mom, and in almost a tackle motion grabbed me and hugged me so very tight. I can say that this action and also felt so right to me.

I told him, "Thanks, Rocky, but we have to go now. Dad and I need to go and get a hurt dog that had been in an accident with me. I will explain later."

Dad interrupted and said, "He appears to be alright, but I need to check out what's going on with this dog right now! We will bring his dog up to the house and get it some help, as Mickey seems to think it's badly injured. We can then see what if anything we can do to help him so that he doesn't suffer."

I had caught my dad's statement when referred to the big dog as if it was indeed already my dog.

He went on by saying, "Please, as Mickey has told you, Rocky, that we'll be right back, and there will be time then to answer any of your questions at that time. So we need to get going and help this big dog out!"

Rocky and Mom just nodded their heads in agreement, and after nodding her approval, she put her arm around Rocky's shoulders and guided him into the house.

Dad turned to lead the way down the pathway. After only a few steps, I stopped him saying, "No, Dad, you don't understand. We will need the big construction wheelbarrow you have because this is a huge dog, and, no kidding, he is almost is as big or bigger than I am."

Dad turned and went over to the garage and returned out with the wheelbarrow, and down the pathway, we went.

By now, it was dark, but I noticed that Dad had stopped long enough to grab a flashlight.

He handed me the flashlight and asked me to lead the way. As we walked down the pathway and what I knew was that it was not very far, but it seemed that it was taking us a long time to get there.

I found from the glow of the flashlight I could just make out the outline of the big dog lying under the big oak right where I had left him. It didn't look like he had moved at all, and, as we approached him, I could not make out if he was even breathing. So as we got closer and closer, I was trying to see if he was even still alive. I noticed as I bent down, placing the beam lower down, and I could see the slight rise of his chest.

It was then that I saw the burn down his back and noticed the smell of burned fur again. This smell caused a flashback to when that odor had come rushing into my senses when I had found the big dog lying on top of me earlier.

I silently chuckled to myself as I remembered my first evaluation of the animal on top of me, thinking it might be a bear. I wondered whatever made me even think of a bear. Then I remembered that a few nights ago I had seen a TV show where a man who had gone to Alaska to live with bears, and eventually they ate him. This chilling thought made me cringe. Then it was not so confusing when I had thought it through.

Now there he was, and we could see a jagged line about three to four inches wide that had been laid bare of skin and fur, and these spots looked like the spots were weeping and appeared that they would have been very painful had the dog had been awake.

The area, where the coat and skin were burnt off, was so clean that one would think that a knife had done the removal.

But the smell of burned flesh and hair told that something had burned this off. I thought about a floor burn I got once in basketball, and I could remember just how much it hurt every time I had to bend my knee until it scabbed over. The dog's wound looked ten times worse than my floor burn had.

With the flashlight focused on the wound, we could see that it started at his front paws then around to the dog's back we could see that the removal of fur then went down the dogs back in a zigzagging pattern down to the dogs tail where it split and ran along both sides of his tail. Then it traveled down the backside of both hind legs. I could see that his front and back paw pads are all severely burned as well.

It was very dark now as clouds even prevented the moon from showing any light. The threat of rain darkened my thoughts even more.

I marveled at my father's wisdom because we would now be in total darkness, were it not for the flashlight.

I was so proud of my father 's wisdom; I felt that he could solve any problem that I might bring to him.

And for some reason, another feeling passed through my mind; I could not explain it. I just knew that the big dog was going to be all right. And somehow the big dog was going to be in my life. Then my thoughts centered on the question of where had this big dog come from today?

Dad made a whistling sound and said, "Son, you weren't kidding about the fact that this was one big dog. The second fact is you weren't kidding about him being badly hurt!"

I said, "Thanks, Dad, for believing me, and being willing to help with him."

Dad stopped and looked at me, pausing to impress the effect of his words. Then went on and said, "Mickey, you have always been honest with me. So, I have always been able to trust what you have told me. So now you can see just how important the truth is."

When he finished his comments, he quickly turned back to the task at hand of getting the dog into the wheelbarrow.

He stood back up and then reached over and grabbed me to give me a big hug and said, "Son, I love you very, very much, and I want you to know how very, very proud of you, I am!"

I smiled at him, but my thoughts then flashed back to how selfish I have been in the last few days because of the move. And the problems I had caused by dragging my feet about it all. Then and there, I decided to change my attitude. I felt for the first time since I found out that we had to move, I found that all that guilt was now gone. I was no longer worried about abandoning my buddies back home.

My thoughts then flashed to and about Becky, as I have decided that I know that I was truly home here. I also knew that she had played a large part in my change of my mind on liking it here.

I thought for a second as I asked myself, was this not what books, and movies, call love that I feel right now? I then thought I'm too young to be worried about this. These mixed feelings were about to drive me nuts.

I felt an overwhelming need to get her something to let her know that she is more than just a friend to me.

Dad was looking at me funny and asked, "Are you alright?" When I nodded yes, he then asked, "Will you lift my end a little more so that we can keep him as level as possible while putting him into the wheelbarrow."

So, I turned back to the task at hand of keeping my thoughts focused on my helping to keep the big dogs head level. I know that it was not that my dad was unable to lift this big dog all by himself, but I felt from his statement that he just wanted not to hurt him any more than was needed.

Dad confirmed my thoughts when he asks me, "Please help to stabilize as much as you can to keep the neck straight when we pick him up.

I then brought my thoughts to the big dog as I could now tell that he was a little bigger than the big construction wheelbarrow was in length.

Dad was pushing it up the path towards the house. I was walking beside the wheelbarrow, and, while walking sideways, I was trying to keep up, and, at the same time, lift the big dog's head and make his head stable and level. I was having somewhat of a hard time because I found it hard to try and keep up. While at the same time keeping the flashlight focused, and to top it off while at the same time trying to keep the big dogs head level.

Dad, in his wisdom, had asked Mom to bring a clean blanket outside that we could make into a makeshift stretcher. He spread it out on the lawn and then placed the dog on the sheet. Then Dad showed us how to roll up the edges of the sheet, and I found that this gave us all something to grip as we lifted the big dog. He then asked us to take the rolled-up edges of the blanket, and we found that it was then more comfortable to be able to divide the big dog's weight between the three of us, helping to make it easy to lift the big dog then. It worked super, and soon, we were easily carrying him through the back door.

Upon entering the kitchen, I could see that Mom had been very busy while we were gone. She had cleared off the table, as Dad had asked her to do. She not only did that but had also moved the table to the center of the room. We now brought it in and set the dog on it, so it was directly below the kitchen light.

In the better view from the better light of the kitchen, we could now see the full damage of the massive burn. We could see the path as it did indeed run from the dog's front paws down front legs and around the dog's neck on both sides. The blaze had then traveled down the middle of the big dog's back. It had then traveled down to both hind legs. It continued down to both rear paws, as we had earlier observed. Now I could see that the burns looked even worse than they had appeared in the dimmer light of the flashlight.

With the big dog resting on the table peacefully, I felt like I could relax a little. The strong nauseating smell of burned hair and flesh came rushing to my senses once again.

Dad and Mom began to wash the area of his burns, and that was when Dad told us to stop. He looked at Mom and said, "Honey, we need to stop and get the vet out here to take a look at this animal because we want to do this right."

Mom nodded her head in approval of that thought.

Dad stepped over to the wall phone that was hanging on the kitchen wall. There was the number written on a card that had several numbers on it. Dad said, "I thought I had seen the name of a veterinarian on it earlier. And here it is." He dialed, and we could only hear one side of the conversation. But it was clear to me that the vet had answered. When he was through talking on the phone, he hung up and told us, "The vet was helping the Smith family down the road a short way with a cow that was having problems birthing a calf. He told me he was just leaving and would be here in a few minutes."

While we were waiting for the vet, Dad used this time to ask me, "Are you really alright, son?"

I looked at him, saying, "Yes, I feel just fine except for the burn I feel on both sides of my chest." Dad asks, "Burn on your chest? What burns on your chest? You didn't even mention burns before when I asked you the same question earlier."

Dad and Mom both stepped quickly across to where I stood, staring in unison, "Pull up your t-shirt."

I reached down and, for the first time, saw the two perfect paw prints. It was burned a lot worse than any simple sunburn. We could all see that bad blisters had formed on each side.

Dad and Mom both looked at my chest then back at the dog's paws. Dad finally said, "Mickey, I have never seen anything like that in my life." Mom put some ointment on my chest that she had been using on the dog earlier.

She then asks, "Did he do this to you?"

I just shrugged my shoulders and said, "Mom, I don't know what happened, I just woke up, and he was on top of me. I was out cold, and as I told you, I don't remember anything."

We could hear the vet's pickup coming up the driveway. I walked over to the door, opened it, and found that he was already out of his truck walking toward our back door. He was carrying a little black medical bag, and as he entered, he introduced himself, "I'm your local vet, Doc Jones." Dad walked past me to where the short man stood and said, "Thanks for coming out at this late hour," and reached out to shake his hand as he thanked him. Doc Jones shook Dad's hand and shrugged off the apology, saying, "No problem, Mr. Turner, as I told you I was just on my way home from helping your neighbors with their cow birthing that calf."

After the formalities were over, he repeated what he had said earlier, "Absolutely no problem, Mr. Turner, I do whatever I can to help hurt animals. Let's see what we have here and exactly what we can do to help this big guy. Boy, he is hurt," he said. He then asked, "What happened?"

Dad explained, just as I had told him. Then with that, Dad pulled up my t-shirt, exposing my chest, and there were the burns with the blistering appearing to be not as bad as when we had all looked only a few minutes before. The Vet looked at my bare chest and paused for a moment, and seeing the perfect paw print on each side of my chest just below my collarbone plain as day.

He then exclaimed excitedly, "I know what happened. You know that lightning storm we had today?" Pointing to my chest. He went on, "I have seen this a hundred times when I have to go out and help a farmer with cattle or horses were standing under a tree when that tree had a lighting strike hit the tree, they usually do not survive."

He continued, "While your son was touching the tree, the dog sensed that lightning was going to strike your boy; he jumped, putting his paws on your son's chest, knocking him off his feet. While this dog's paws were still in contact with your son, the lightning bolt passed through them both. In this way, your boy's feet were not in contact with the ground. Doc then pointed towards the big dog lying on the table, saying, "I believe that this big boy here took the full brunt of that lightning strike as he did have his rear paws still in contact with the ground. I think that he did all this at the same time the lightning struck the tree. If Mickey here had had both his feet on the ground, I think he would be dead. As I have said, I feel that this dog more than likely saved your son's life, Mr. and Mrs. Tanner!"

I heard Mom gasp, then she reached out and touched the burn spots on my chest very lovingly. She then looked at the big dog lying there, and she reached out while touching me she stroked the big dog's fur. The way she looked at the dog was completely different now. I felt that it was a look of great love for the big black dog. Tears started to form, and then began to flow as she stroked the dog's fur even more lovingly.

I noticed that Dad's attitude began to soften and change, as well. Now it seemed he was even more attentive and was showing a softer side as he assisted Doc Jones in dressing the black dog's wounds.

Dad finally asked what no one had stated out loud, "Doc, do you know who this dog belongs to?"

Doc Jones looked at him but paused as if thinking. He looked back at the dog again, then said, "Well, Mr. Hunter, I have never met the man who I think owns the dog. But all that I hear about him is that he is more than just mean to his dogs. I've only seen him in town occasionally buying supplies. There's a rumor that the man fights dogs in pit fights. It is just a rumor, and I can't prove this, you see, because neither the sheriff or the state police have been able to catch him in the act."

Doc continued by saying. "I just drove by his driveway coming from the Smith's farm. His place is less than a mile down the road on the right." He pointed toward the road with his thumb to the right. He said, "If you go up to his place, watch yourselves. Just remember to protect yourselves as the man is said to be truly evil."

"Dad, can we keep him?" I asked. I was caressing the dog's coat with even more love than had filled my heart earlier today when I had first rolled him off me out by the big oak tree. The reason was because I now believed that he had saved my life.

Dad said, "We'll have to see tomorrow, son. He belongs to someone else. It is out of our hands at this point."

My heart raced at the thought; he hadn't said no, and that was a good sign. But it was a chilling thought that this beautiful black dog might not be mine brought pain to my heart; that went way beyond anything I had ever felt in my whole life for any animal.

Dad said, "Mickey, I think it would be alright if you and I go over tomorrow and see just what Mr. Billings has to say, since it's Saturday, I don't have to go to work."

A good feeling came over me, and for some reason, I felt ever so strong that this great black dog would somehow become part of our family. For the life of me, I don't know how I could be so sure of this fact, but for some reason, I just knew it.

Dad and Doc Jones finished up bandaging the dog, and Dad asked Doc Jones, "Can you help me get him into Mickey's room?" He answered, "It would be my privilege to help you." Dad and Doc Jones took both corners of the sheet and rolled up the edges to move the dog. They used the sheet as a stretcher, and they gently walked the dog to my room while Dad led the way walking backward. They placed the big dog gently on the floor at the side of my bed.

I could hear them talking for a while in the living room. My dad asked, "Doc Jones, would you please bill me for treating the dog?" Then there was silence.

I lay on my bed with the door shut, and my lamp lit. I just sat there looking down at the dog. Then the thought crossed my mind, if I get to keep the dog, what will I name it? The name Lightning came quickly to mind. Since the big dog saved me from a lightning strike, therefore, what better name than Lightning. I wished that I could just wake this big dog up and ask him what had happened, and have him be able to answer me, wouldn't that be something to talk about!

But I do realize talking to animals was a good story, and a Dr. Doolittle-type story is only a dream for the very young at heart.

I know that it could never actually happen. But I thought if only the dog could talk, I bet he would have quite a story to tell.

What if we had not moved to this small town of Ridgefield, north of Vancouver, WA. I would never have known Becky or Biff, or matter of fact, I would never have even known Lightning either.

Then I felt guilty and knew that I would need to make up for my actions and spoiled acts of the last few days about the move here.

I then looked at my bare chest and saw the blistered burns, where Lightning's paws had struck me and ultimately saved my life.

Earlier tonight, after cleaning up the big dog, they then took great pains to tend to the burns on my chest. I looked at the bandages that Doc Jones had placed over each one and was surprised at how well the tape kept the bandages so secure to keep the ointment my mom had put there from being held in place and not coming off. I marveled at the great job Doc Jones had done.

Even though the spots still hurt, but the pain was almost gone. But I wouldn't be sleeping on my chest anytime soon. A sudden good feeling swept through my body, and there was a feeling of pride that Lightning and I do share something, even if it was only a burn.

Then I thought back to what Doc Jones had said earlier about the burns would probably leave scars. The scars from where Lightning's paws had touched and burned me would become my badge of courage and my bond between him and me.

After eating a sandwich, I went into the bathroom and brushed my teeth. I made a point of telling each of my parents, just how much I liked being here. I also apologized for being such a pain about the move here. They both gave me a hug and a kiss on the cheek. I knew then that they had forgiven me.

I went back into my bedroom to see if I could get some sleep.

As I lay on my back in bed, I found that I had to lie that way because lying on my side caused my arms to push up on my chest, and that hurt. So I just lay there staring at the ceiling.

I finally leaned forward slightly, looking down at Lightning lying on a blanket next to my bed and centered my attention on the big dog. I watched him breathe and reached over to pet him, and I felt a great feeling come over me and knew two things, first that he was going to be all right. The second feeling was that he was going to be mine. I couldn't see how that was to be, but I knew with no doubt in my mind that he will be with me.

I woke with a start because my hand was wet from a big sloppy kiss from the big black dog standing over me. With the shadows cast by my bedside lamp, the dog looked incredibly menacing standing over me.

He just stood there watching me. I was so afraid because I didn't remember him immediately. Fear was ruling my actions, and before I could even think straight, I just simply rolled off the bed on the other side. As my feet hit the floor, I crossed the floor at a fast pace. I looked back at him, and he hadn't moved, but instead just sat there looking at me.

The lights from the lamp made him appear more massive than before. The dog cast shadows on my wall that were almost eerie.

I was just opening the door when I heard something, and I stopped halfway out the door. A clear voice said, "Don't be afraid." It was not being said out loud like regular voices. The sound was like no other that I had ever heard. It was low-pitched and very soothing, and even though it was a soft voice, it came through just loud enough to be heard. I looked around the room to see who was trying to play a joke on me.

I then started focusing on what it was saying.

The voice said, "It's me."

I then realized that for sure, there was no doubt that it was just a voice coming into my mind. It was calming to me, but at the same time, I thought that maybe I was losing my mind. Now I wondered if the shock I received today caused me to lose my mind.

Then the voice came through again ever so softly, saying again, "Please don't be afraid, it's me, and to answer your question, no, you are not losing your mind."

I looked around the room until I was sure there was no one else in the room. I was halfway in and halfway out of the room. I was still somewhat scared, but on the other hand, there was indeed a feeling of excitement of this was like being an unknown adventure.

I dropped my eyes down to the big dog just sitting there very quietly as if to let the fact that I could hear him sink in.

I would swear the dog was smiling at me. I thought this must be a joke; no one can read a dog's mind. I searched the room once more, seeing that there was still no one else in the room but the dog and me.

I shook my head, trying to clear my mind. When that voice came through loud and clear again, "Yes, Mickey, it's me! I am giving you my thoughts by way of our minds. There is nothing wrong with your mind."

After I had calmed down, I sat back on the bed staring at the big black dog. I couldn't believe what was happening, and it was happening way to fast, but then a calm came over me that I had never felt in my life before.

I rose to get my mom and dad and tell them that the dog was now awake and the exciting news that I can read this dog's mind, and that thought excited me.

Then I heard the voice again, "No, you don't want to let anyone know that you can read my mind." I was very disappointed because I had a gift, and I wanted to tell my family and friends just what I could do.

"What would you think, Mickey, if someone told you they could read a dog's mind? And if they find out that you think you can understand me and hear you say that you can hear me, they will think that you are losing your mind for sure."

I started to speak out loud, as that is the way that I am used to communicating. He stopped me mentally, telling me if they go by the door and hear you talking to a dog, they might start calling the Funny Farm, remember. Again, they tend to figure something is wrong with any person who thinks that they could be possible talking with animals.

He lay back down on the sheet that Dad and Doc had brought him into my bedroom on.

I could tell that he was very, very tired but he told me, "No, I want to talk to you and let you know about the way it once was. Man, and dogs used to have an equal relationship we hunted together. I can say, Mickey, we were a formidable team together back then. We could talk to each other mentally, like telepathy. The dogs and my big brother, the wolf, were all part of the team. The bond was because we trusted the humans who got along with us. Some of the dogs in the animal world loved man so much that they went to live with them.

We took care of each other. The dogs protected the tribes and helped man hunt for food. The dogs became guardians for man's family's warning them of impending danger, and many, many times, gave up their lives to protect their adopted families.

Like I told you, there was a trust back then, but when the white man came into the picture, the trust began to fade. The Indians could no longer practice the old ways, and the white men had them sent to schools that frowned on the old ways and the old beliefs. We found that in the end, all the Indians lost their belief in the old ways. You can say that Indians lost the gift of being able to talk to the animals. That ability to converse with us was lost right along with the ability to change into animal form and along with several other things.

This ability, along with the teamwork that used to be between us, we were unable to hunt together and protect each other. These gifts we all held became a lost art.

Many, many white men and red men alike have wanted to return to the old ways. Every time the council approved of someone, we thought worthy, but when put to the test, they have always failed. Up until now, the chosen have never had the intelligence or the mindset that matches yours.

I'm not saying we haven't tried to get some people, and my prior owner is an example of such an attempt that went wrong. We found after trying it with him that he turned so utterly evil. You are our next try, and I am to say that you need to know that it all rests with you, my friend.

Mickey, I am the controller of the gifts you hold. We are the holders of the keys to communicate, are held accountable, and so you are to answer to me.

If you abuse the gifts in any way and you are unable to be willing to change. I must take them from you, and you will never even remember that you held them.

We, the controllers, had about given up hope that someone worthy would come along.

And now you are here. I have passed all the keys on to you, and we must take the time together for you to learn of their awesome power. So, my friend, you need to know the tremendous good that you can do with these gifts. What we have found, unlike the people of old, that the humans of today get the gifts they let greed rule them. They then become caught up in power and become unwilling to change. It is our hope as controllers that we have been able to learn a lesson or two, and now with you to get you a better training program and therefore make the gifts work the way that it is supposed to.

For you to learn how to use all these new gifts you have, I need for you to understand all your gifts. It will take a while to complete all the training. I will cover and add to the list of gifts you have as they are needed. You will find that after a certain period, you will become able to call upon many of the added gifts on your own. We think this is because of how smart and pure of heart you are, my friend.

You will always have the right to refuse to keep these gifts, because no force will ever make you use these gifts, my friend.

You need to feel comfortable with each of the gifts as you get them and learn about them slowly. The keys that are in you were passed on to you when we were both struck by lightning.

I felt that the lightning was going to strike you, and when I saw that you were about to die, I felt forced to move quicker on my plan to give the gifts to you. I also knew that the lightning strike would make the passing stronger and faster. So, my friend, I made a snap decision, and so here we are. I am your teacher, and I alone am responsible for your education in the use of the keys.

I will teach you the real power of all the keys you have. I say again, to strengthen the warning, many others before you have had a hard time not to let greed take over. So, now from me to you, all the gifts have been restored to their fullness. All of our hopes are resting on you, Mickey. It is the hope that we will be able to rein in a new era of helping both men and animals.

With you, we, the keepers of the keys, decided to try something different this time. And so, my friend, we are with you a much younger person this time. It would appear to us that you would be able to handle the powers given because of just how smart you are.

There is another point that you need to know is that we, the controllers and holder of the keys, cannot use them. Only humans are empowered to use the gifts; we are only able to give, take away, and to teach about the keys.

We have missed the relationship that only the dogs and wolves of old remember, and they pass the stories onto the young ones. But in these modern times, we have never had the same type of relationship. None have been able to stay worthy long enough to even learn of all the miraculous gifts they held. I ask you to use their gifts for only good.

Until you came along, we had almost given up hope.

Before the lightning strike, I saw you when you moved in, and was watching you. I was able to assess your spirit and down to your very soul. I can say that never have I seen any person with such a pure heart.

A chill ran down my spine. I was overwhelmed at being chosen for this blessing.

I still needed to ask, "Why me? I'm only twelve years old,"

We in the dog kingdom never lost the skill of reading minds. That is because no one brainwashed us into giving up our miraculous gifts. We were able to expand our learning through men's minds. Using those thoughts gave us ideas, knowledge, and better words, and the way that humans used those words furthered our knowledge. So my friend, because we were able to hear men's thoughts. We were then able to learn from all humans we were ever around throughout all time.

I wanted you to know that my kind was thrilled to hear that the chosen one was found and is now about to enter into training.

We, the controllers, now feel that you and I will be able to create a successful bonding that, in the end, be helpful to all humanity and animals alike. The controllers felt that the Great Spirits intended this for all.

The council felt that maybe you and I would be the first to succeed, especially since I had to take back the gifts just a few years ago from the man you know as Billings.

I feel that I need to remind you, Mickey, that you can never tell anyone about these restored gifts. As I stated earlier, the outside world will think you have lost your mind if you were to tell others that you can talk to a dog. You will want to speak of it, but no one can ever know unless I, your controller, have cleared it.

There are only two more things that I need to let you know right now. The first is that I like the name Lightning you gave me, because it was indeed lightning that started this off.

With the load of information I was given, I was almost overwhelmed. So, I lay back down, looked at Lightning, and went to sleep.

But just before nodding off, I thought of my friends back home. I must admit that I still would like to see the old gang, but I didn't want to leave Ridgefield now.

CHAPTER NINE

MY GIFTS

I awoke, and as I slipped out of bed, I remembered that this was Saturday.

I looked at the clock, and I realized I had slept in a little. It was almost noon. I must have been a lot more tired than I thought last night.

I thought about my new friends, Biff and the gang of football players. I thought it would be fantastic if my old buddies were here to share my good times. But at the same time, I know that it could never happen.

I also thought about the new house, and I had to admit that I do genuinely love it here.

I had to admit that the reason I liked my new home and school was mainly because of my new and wired feelings that I have for Becky.

Before leaving my room, I checked on Lightning and saw that he was just fine. I left my room and headed down the hallway toward the kitchen. I needed to see who was up and about. I needed to find Dad. I figured that he is usually an early riser and would more than likely be sitting at the breakfast nook reading the newspaper.

I felt a new surge of energy and wanted to get started making Lightning mine. I am a kid on a mission.

As I entered the kitchen, I found that all three of them were talking.

Dad greeted me with, "Hi Mickey, we have been waiting for you to get up so we can go and see that man about Lightning." Mom then said, "Your father, and I checked on you a couple of times last night because we have been somewhat worried about you being alright. A lot happened to you yesterday and last night. It's not every day anyone is struck by lightning and survives. As your parents, we feel we have a right to worry. So how do you feel this morning?"

Without even thinking, I reached up and touched my chest. I noticed the burns weren't painful at all. If anything, they itched a little that made me believe they were healing very fast.

As if that was a signal to check, Mom walked over and pulled up my t-shirt. She said, "You know, honey, I think that is going to leave a scar," but in almost the same breath, she said, "Mark look at just how fast Mickey has healed." Dad came over and said, "Yeah, those scars are going to be your badge of courage."

He then said jokingly, "Those scars are also going to drive the girl's nuts and look at how it's the perfect paw print of the big dog!"

He smiled at me, and I knew that I must be blushing because my face was hot. He then reached up and ruffled my hair with his big hand.

I thought immediately about Becky, and I was wondering just what she would think about these new scars, or if they would even bother her at all.

For some unexplained reason, I see in my mind's eye, that when Lightning's wounds healed, his new fur would come back in white, not black like the rest of his body. I looked closer through my mind's eye, and I could now see just how Lightning's burns were going to heal and scar. I can see quite clearly now that his new white fur will resemble a lightning strike down his back.

My first thought was that each of us would carry a scar that will bond us forever together, me with the perfect paw prints and Lightning with a white strip down his back.

A question flashed quickly through my mind was being able to see into the future one of the gifts I received? Then I questioned further, was the picture correct with Lightning having white fur when he healed?

I'm looking forward to being able to see if indeed his coat returns with a white blaze down his back or not.

I wondered about what Doc Jones had said that Mr. Billings might be more than a little reluctant to give up such a prize dog.

But at the base of my brain was that Lightning would be mine today.

I just have not had the added vision on exactly tell me just how this will be able to take place. But when my feelings are running so strong that for some reason, it will happen without a doubt.

But doubt now entered my mind bringing about one central question, if Lightning was such a valuable fighting dog, why would Billings ever be willing to give him up?

I rushed back into the bedroom, and it was a real surprise when Lightning began to answer the questions that had just crossed my mind.

His first answer was, "Yes, this man Billings is so very, very cruel way beyond the worst idea you can imagine; and yes, he does fight dogs. But that is only one of the big shows that he puts on."

I felt a pain that seemed to shoot through my heart to hear that there were people who could even possibly treat any animal that way, and all for money.

Lighting went on, "Mickey, the essential thing to me about the fights was that they were fights to the death."

"Billings felt that he couldn't afford to keep an animal that was not willing to fight and make him money. So we fought to survive. The very worst thing I ever had to do was when I had to be in a pit against my very own brother!"

"My brother made me kill him because I was the holder of the keys, and he knew that my survival was a must. This fact did not help me feel any better about what I had to do, though."

I asked Lightning, "Do you think that Billings will ever give you up?" He answered emphatically, "NO, because I am his very best fighter and remember when I told you that most humans couldn't handle the gifts. The reason I say this is because greed always enters in once the holder gets the keys to the gifts. In days of old, that was not the case because humans acted with love when they used the keys."

Lightning then went on, "You see, Billings was once a holder of the keys of all the gifts you now hold. I can say that at the time they were given to him, he was a very nice and peaceful person. I had to remove the keys and, therefore, the gifts from his presence. I found out that when I wiped out his memory of even holding the keys. He became an even crueler man. He is the real example of just how wrong we sometimes can be in reading you, humans. When he slipped over to the dark side, and I removed the keys, it was like he ripped my spirit in two. I felt betrayed, and it took me many months to recover. I even started to doubt the need to have a human ever be a holder of the keys anymore. But then there was a change in my heart when I saw into your pure heart, Mickey."

Then he stopped and said, "I feel that you know something, don't you, Mickey?" He went on to answer his question after I nodded yes. And even before he could answer, I said, "I can see in your mind that I will be with you from now on, won't I?"

His tail began to wag very fast. Then he stopped moving his tail and said, "Boy, it hurts a lot when I wag my tail right where the burn goes around my tail." I thought, "I am so sorry that you're in so much pain because of me, but at the same time, I am so glad that you thought enough of me to risk your life."

His thoughts had come in so fast, and so clear at the same time, it was loud. It was almost like he was yelling at me.

As Lightning went on, "I'd do it again in a minute because I love you. And you know I have already told you, Mickey, that you are the chosen one, and I know that you are supposed to have the gifts you now hold. I also know with no doubt that you will be the servant of all living things that need help because of that big soft and pure heart of yours."

He continued, "I know that the other gifts that you have received from me will lay dormant until the need arises, and at that time, you will instinctively know what they are and how to use them. I will be there to explain and teach only when you might not understand. You will not even know that you have the gifts until they are needed. Yet my friend, when the time is rights these gifts, with, their awesome powers will be yours to control."

He stopped and looked at me and waited for a second or two then he said, "Yes, you are correct the gift of seeing into the future is yours, my friend. You will find that if you turn this gift on all the time, you will then find that it will bore you. The reason you will become bored is because you will know everything that is about to happen. So as a suggestion, turn it off until you need it for real, you will be a lot happier. As I have told you before, you are also the youngest holder of the keys. When you use your understanding, along with your willingness to help others, you will find then that you will be able to unlock the fullness of your powers. And the abilities you now possess will then become more vigorous and more natural the more you use them. You will then find yourself to be a very, very powerful young man. Please don't do it for the glory that will surely come anyway, but to be able to right wrongs and be ready to serve everyone and everything for the good of all. I only tell you this in passing is to mentally prepare you so that you won't turn to the darker side of man. There is one point that we need to cover, and that is when others want to pay you for the services rendered. The decision on being able to receive is in two parts, first, did it come freely from them or were they pressured to give; second is the ability to pay, and what I mean by this point and to further understand to prevent the misuse of your gifts. If, for instance, a poor person were to need your services, they shall not be required to pay."

"You see, Mickey, these gifts are sacred to us. We believe that it is a terrible wrong to see them used in any way other than the ways that the Great Spirit intended for their usage. Each time the gifts must be taken back from anyone that we thought was worthy. We find the act of removing them crushes our hearts every time."

"We feel that never has there been a time in history when the need for a spiritual leader has ever been more needed. So here we are, Mickey, standing at the crossroads of the most significant restoration since the gifts have ever given."

"I hope and pray that when that time comes that you will be ready to saddle this responsibility and be able to ride it to the desired end."

A shiver went down my spine at the thought of what I had just heard. I feel that the shiver was my spirit, witnessing the truthfulness of Lightnings statements.

"Mickey, you are already incredibly smart, but now one of the gifts is an even higher level of understanding of the power of the gifts you now possess. We desire that this added wisdom you will become many years older than your actual age."

"Also, one of the other gifts given is that of an extended life span, so to understand this to say it simply, you will age much slower than other humans. Follow your gut when you have a strong feeling, follow it. You will find that if you have no greed in your heart or wrong motive to the act, you are fine to go with it."

Lightning continued, "So, my friend, when you finished with all of your training, you will have become the most powerful human to have existed since the time of Merlin, the Magician."

It was then that I could hear my dad coming down the hallway. There was a feeling that came over me that I realized just what Lightning had talked about earlier. I felt that I was to help Lightning right now.

And before my dad could open my bedroom door, I quickly followed that prompting of my heart, I reached out and petting Lightning on the head so Dad would never suspect what I was doing.

As soon as my hands touched his head, a small bolt of blue electricity traveled to my fingertips. The movement caused a tingling sensation in my fingers, and I found this sensation wasn't painful at all. It sort-of tickled. I quickly ran my fingers down his back, and the bolt of energy followed my hands. As I continued down, the blue bolt danced from my fingers to his back and back again. I went all the way down to the burns at the very bottom of all four of his paws.

Lightning let out a sigh of relief. His thoughts came through so clear, "Thanks, Mickey! You have no idea of what a relief that I feel. I find because of what you have just done, and I am now pain-free! You are now a healer, my friend. Healing is one of the gifts you currently have. You handled it very well."

When he told me this, I can say that I never can remember having had this kind of rush of pure joy that seemed to touch my heart.

My spirit had kicked into overdrive, and that feeling was something I wanted to be with me all the time.

I could hear Lightning telling me that this is the feeling I could expect to have when I do something special to help another in need. I can say that no amount of money can ever buy this feeling.

My thought now was if I get this kind of feeling every time I use the gifts, I would have been willing to pay someone for the right to help others just to receive this type of high.

I looked up and saw that my dad was standing in my bedroom doorway, and I thought back quickly if I had heard him knock. I was sure in my mind that he probably did.

I knew that we have always had the rule of absolute privacy.

I feel that because I was so deep in my thoughts was the real reason that I was unable to hear Dad enter.

The main question I ask myself right now was just exactly how much had he seen or heard?

I wanted in the worst way to tell both of my parents all about the gifts. I also wanted them to know about the high I get when I use those gifts.

It was then that Lightning's came back into the center of my mind as he reminded me, "Once again, I have found a need to remind you, my friend, of the inability to tell anyone unless it is pre-approved.

The forgetfulness made me upset with myself for my short-term memory loss.

I remembered in that instant, that for us to do our job correctly in the future, total secrecy needed to be first on my list every day twenty-four/seven.

That thought made me feel a little sad, as I had always been able to share everything with my parents. The idea of that thought that I might never be able to share with them about the gifts, I find that thought was somewhat saddened me even more.

I noticed that he had a funny look on his face as he walked across the floor. He looked down at Lightning and said out loud, "That is something!"

I ask, "What do you mean, Dad?" thinking he had found out someway about our secret.

He looked up at me and said, "I have never seen a nasty burn like his heal this fast."

I then turned my attention once again to Lightning's burns and noticed that his injuries had already scabbed over. I could remember what Doc. Jones had told us that the wound this bad would take from seven to ten days to heal, or possibly even much longer.

He looked at it and said, "Look, the burns have already scabbed over, and it looks to be healing well." He noted, "Even the bottom of his paws showing signs of fast healing all over."

To try and turn his thoughts away from me, I quickly said, "It must have been the ointment that Doc Jones and my mom put on him that caused him to heal so much faster."

Lightning thoughts passed to me, "Great job, quick thinking and with that thought planted, and it will cover up the fact that it was you that healed me. It will stop unneeded questions that would have been difficult to answer."

And he agreed with my thoughts and told me further, "It does not matter how sad it makes you, you shall never be able to pass on the information to share with your family or anyone else unless cleared first. From now on, my friend, our allegiance of silence, is of a higher order."

I had forgotten for a second that Lightning could read my thoughts.

"Your cover will be protected as you will use the idea of the lightning strike as it has triggered you to now be able to use more of your brain, so you now have a new gift of ESP." I answered, "yes, I remember in some class, the teacher told us that man only uses about five to ten percent of his brain. So using this idea, just maybe we can pull this idea off. The ploy will let me explain a possible idea and then make that idea work and who could prove otherwise. That will take any idea that you had anything to do with this newfound ability. Now we can explain to people how the lightning strike opened my ability to use more of my mind, and now I have the power of ESP. I went on, "Lightning this will give people an answer to my new abilities as they look for something to believe in is all that is needed. As I said, "No one can prove otherwise, my friend. Our secret should be safe. The idea will be an explanation that I think people will buy into a new idea. When the time is right, I will drop this for all to hear; now we have a game plan."

I received no response from that thought from Lightning, so I choose not to worry about it right now. The plan will make some people curious about your newfound abilities, but they already have been told that some can hold the powers of ESP. The idea of ESP is not new, and it will, at the same time, head off questions that may arise.

He then passed on to me, "And that my friend is not a lie because that is, in essence, what happened. It just does not go on into detail of the full picture of the gifts that you hold. The plan will shelter the truth and for the protection of our gifts."

He told me one more thing that was almost overwhelming, "Oh yes, one more important thing is that you should remember is that one of the gifts you have received is the one that adds to your strength level. You see, my friend, you now have a unique ability to have at your need; the ability to call upon superhuman strength. It is not always there only when you feel the need to keep you or others out of harm's way. All you need to do is will it, and it will be so. It has always been this way with this gift so that when you are playing games with others, you will not hurt anyone unnecessarily."

My dad nodded his head in agreement with my suggestion of the medication being the healer. Dad went on to further demonstrate his acceptance of the idea, "I need to get some of that medicine to have around here for accidents we might have in the future."

I now know that I will be able to bring forward my gifts anytime they are needed.

CHAPTER TEN

THE ENCOUNTER WITH MR. BILLINGS

Dad was surprised when Lightning was able to jump up into the back of the pickup on his own. He said, "I can't believe the shape he is in now, after seeing him last night, just look at him now. He's doing fantastic!"

We piled into the pickup truck, and off we went.

We cruised slowly down the road looking for Mr. Billing's mailbox. We found it just like Doc had said, "It was just down the road about three miles."

Dad didn't know that Lightning was letting me know exactly where we were, and I simply passed that information along as if it was coming from the directions that Doc Jones had given us. I verbally redirected Lightning's thoughts to my dad as if they were my own.

I looked through the back window of dad's pickup truck watching Lightning as he slumped down as flat as he could when we turned down Billing's lane. Upon reading Lightning's mind, I could understand the fear that Lightning was feeling right now.

Then I passed on to Lightning of my reassurance that he should not worry, that I know down deep that it will somehow end positively.

The fact of the matter is that I just did not know exactly how it would play out to be able to get to my desired end.

Lightning counters with, "I heard what you told me and what worries me so much is you don't know this man like I do. All I can say, my friend, be very careful."

I ask him, "Who was it that told me that I was the holder of the great gifts, and with these gifts comes mighty power? Who told me that, and now is questioning that which you gave them to me?"

I told him, "You must stay strong; we need positive feelings here."

Lightning came back with reassurance, "You are right, I forgot for a moment. But Mickey, I do warn you with the fact that this man is a very, bad man!"

I told Lightning, "Thanks for the warning, but I have powerful gifts, and these powers have not been around for quite some time, you know."

We traveled on down a crooked lane that was rough and full of potholes. Dad's comment was, "I'll bet Doc is right that Mr. Billings doesn't have very many visitors by looking at this road. This road does not lend itself to having other people even to want to come here."

Finally, we rounded a turn, and there was a very rundown shack.

Even before we stepped out of the pickup truck, a man came out of the shack, and I figured he was the very man who we had come to see. Then from the pickup bed, Lightning confirmed my thoughts. Dad bailed out on his side of the truck, and I bailed out of the right side soon after Dad did. We proceeded across the front yard toward the man.

As we got closer, the man's eyes that made me feel so uncomfortable. This man meant business, and the shotgun he cradled in his left arm gave credence to that fact.

He squinted with the meanest look I had ever seen any person give to another.

His dirty clothes did not look like this man had not changed in a month of Sundays, which did not help my evaluation of him one bit.

We had no more than exited the truck, and when we could hear a voice that was almost a snarl, "What do you want here?" Even before we could answer, he spoke even louder and angrier, "Do you not realize that you are on private property, and you have to know that you are trespassing, don't you?"

He stated to make another negative point again before we could speak.

He said bluntly," I don't want anything you have to sell, and I have no desire to join any church you might represent or, for matter fact, anything else you might have to offer me. So, get out of here before someone gets hurt!"

He again rearranged the shotgun as a way of making his point clear.

His way of acting did not bother me as much as the shotgun he had cradled in his left arm. He also had a big pistol on his right hip.

My thoughts were of just how miserable this man is.

I could now hear dogs barking outback.

Dad stepped even closer, seeming to be oblivious to the threats this man has made. He was still approaching Mr. Billings, and my dad reached out his hand to shake hands with this man.

Dad did not seem to be intimidated in the least with his statement or his actions. Mr. Billings just stood looking at Dad's hand for a few moments. Then he finally reached out and took Dad's hand and shook it.

Dad said, "My name is Mark Turner. We live down the road at the big "S" turn on the way back into town. I'm sorry for coming unannounced, but I couldn't find a phone number for you, so that I could have called first. We don't need or want anything, but we do have something that I think belongs to you."

My heart sank at Dad's statement.

Then Dad went on, "Well, that's not altogether true, because we think one of your dogs saved my son's life." He paused as if to get the effect he wanted and then went on, "And if you can see your way clear to help us out here, because he saved my boy's life, we would like to have him for my son's sake. In this short time, my son has become rather attached to the big dog. We would be willing to pay the Vet bill and pay a little more for him if you think that is a fair price for the big dog. Mickey would very much like to have the dog, Mr. Billings."

He had made no reply to what my dad had offered.

When Dad saw no response was coming, "Or Mr. Billings, we would be more than willing to discuss any other options that you might think are fair. But first, we need to see if the dog does belong to you."

His eyes seem to light up at that statement, but he did not speak for the longest time.

As he began to walk towards the pickup truck, he reached over and stood up the shotgun against the stump of a tree and continued walking towards the pickup. When I saw him place the shotgun down, I felt some of the pressure leave him. Putting the shotgun down made me feel somewhat better.

I decided to keep my mouth shut and let my dad take control.

I could see Lightning looking over the edge of the pickup bed, and, as we got closer, I could hear Lightning growling softly. The closer we approached, the louder Lightning growled.

I hear Billings say one word, "Blackie," kind of under his breath, and I hear the name rolled off his tongue in almost a snarl.

Lightning then stood up, and what fur he had left on his back was standing up, and his teeth were showing. The growls began to get closer and closer together, and he reared up on the side of the pickup bed and leaned closer toward Billings.

Billings stopped and turned to look at the shotgun, and he reached back down and picked the pistol from his holster on his hip. I responded by moving in between Billings and Lightning, who was now growling even louder.

Billings asked, "What happened to him?"

Dad moved towards Billings and stood in front of me. He handed Billings the bill that Doc Jones had given him. Mr. Billings looked at Doc Jones' bill then behind our backs at Lightning.

I found that my heart was sitting in my throat and beating a mile a minute.

I don't know what came over me, but I knew what I needed to do - I just had to touch the man. So, that is what I did. I stepped quickly around my dad and found the added speed to get to Billings quickly, which startled me.

Billings jumped back some as he reacted to my fast movement. But when he reached up with his left hand to stop me and at the same time, he reached for the big pistol on his hip.

When Billings tried to push me back, I reached out and took his hand, and when I touched him, a blue electric spark came from my fingertips. As the bolt of electricity surged forth, I felt Mr. Billings relax. In that split second, I felt all the anger that was pent up in him leave his body, and he looked into my eyes and said, "Thank you." I saw tears roll down his face, and the old angry person was no more.

I saw when I had touched him that it was the same blue light that I had seen when I was healing Lightning. The only difference was that this time it just entered his body, not dancing on the surface of his skin, as it had done when I healed Lightning.

But the thing that was so remarkable to me was the feeling that was even greater than when I had treated Lightning. I knew I would never be able to explain those fantastic feelings.

He just slumped forward slightly, and he stumbled a little but quickly gained his balance and looked into my eyes. He touched the place on his hand that I had contacted with, then he paused and just stared at me with a softness that gave me another surge of that great feeling that I had felt before.

I felt my father come up behind me. He grabbed my shoulders and tried to push me back. But then my dad stopped trying to move me out of the way. It was as if he suddenly understood that the crisis was over.

I looked at the pistol still in its holster as Billings had not even had time to draw the weapon. We both paused for a moment, and I felt terrific about the part I had played because I felt that warm fuzzy feeling was back again.

Dad and I just stood there looking at who was a new man standing in front of us. His very look has changed, and as we stood looking at Mr. Billings, we saw softer facial features, and all his anger seemed to be gone.

Lightning knew from my thoughts that Mr. Billings wasn't a problem, so he stopped growling.

My dad just stayed in this position behind me, rubbing my upper arms.

Billings looked at me, saying, "What was that all about?" He did not wait for an answer just began to shake his head back and forth as if trying to clear his mind.

I just looked at him, and I repeated, "We just want to have this big dog because we think he saved my life, there are no tricks here as you can check it out. You can look for yourself, and you will see the big blaze down his back, and you will be able to see where the lightning struck him while he was trying to save me."

I went on quickly before he could cut me off, "Could we please work something out; I am willing to come here and work for you to work as long as you want to pay off the bill for him. The main reason that I want to do this is because of what he did for me by saving my life. I believe that you will deal fairly with me. I have a new bike, and I can ride up here and work for you after school and on weekends. If that isn't okay, then I will work somewhere else and pay you with my earnings for what you think he is worth it because I love him, Mr. Billings."

He looked at us and said nothing for the longest time. We both just stood there, silently letting him ponder my words. I was looking into his eyes and let him consider what I have said. I was not sure, but I thought my dad was nodding his approval even though I couldn't see him. Billings didn't say anything for what seemed like forever, but I saw that it was only a few moments.

My thoughts were racing around in my head, but for some reason, they were quite organized at the same time.

My first thought was, did I say enough to find the right key that had unlocked this man's heart?

He finally turned his attention to my father, and then he asked, "Did he save your son's life?" My dad answered, "Yes, he did, Mr. Billings."

Then my father reached up under my arms and lifted my t-shirt, and there was Lightning's paw print very, very visible. Billings asked, "How did that happen?"

Dad then went on to explain what Doc Jones had said about what had happened.

Mr. Billings lowered his eyes, staring at the ground for some time. That was when I knew that we had gotten through to him. My touch had started this man's cold heart to begin to thaw. I now knew that, for me, the scientific tests were over in my mind. This healing of this man's cold heart cinched it. I know now that I am a true healer.

He then looked at me and said, "If you are willing to pay the vet bill and are also willing to give me fifty dollars, then I will consider it a done deal!"

I said, "I can't thank you enough, Mr. Billings."

And with that, my dad pulled out his wallet and counted out two twenties and a ten and handed them to him, and said, "Thank you ever so much, Mr. Billings." The speed with which my dad did this was as if he was afraid that Billings might change his mind.

As Dad backed our pickup up a little so we could turn it around to leave, I waved to Mr. Billings, and he waved back.

Dad looked over at me and said, "You owe me fifty bucks, and you're going to work it out, aren't you?"

I nodded my head, yes, and he reached over and ruffled my hair up, and then looked through the back window at Lightning. He said, "What did you do to that man, son? I saw the turnaround in his actions and his attitude that only changed after you touched him."

I paused not wanting to lie to my father but, on the other hand, not sure of what to say, because Lightning had told me not to tell anyone. So, I didn't answer him right away. I thought about using the explanation Lightning and I had figured out: using "ESP" to answer the question. But I didn't want to lie to my father. So, instead of saying anything, I just shrugged my shoulders and looked down at the floor. Then Lightning and I could figure out the right time to tell my mom and dad about the "ESP."

Shrugging my shoulders felt like a lie because I did know how it had happened, and that bothered me. So I said, "Dad, a lot has happened in the last couple of days that I don't truly understand."

Dad looked at me and said, "I love you, and I'm so very proud of you."

I smiled and reached across the seat and gave him a big hug. He quickly told me, "Put your seatbelt back on." I smiled at him and snapped the belt clasp as loud as I could.

I then let my thoughts run wild as we drove back towards home. My first thought was that I couldn't ever remember feeling this good in my whole life. I looked back at Lightning and found that he was asleep. I thought I was the happiest and luckiest guy in the world. I also wondered what other gifts that were in store for me. I made a note to ask Lightning that question tomorrow; I am way too tired to get into that tonight.

I felt the glow was so intense around me, making me feel on top of the world looking down on the whole of creation. To put it simply, it was a great day, and even though I'm tired, I felt that I had grown in my new calling. After taking a quick shower, I wished Lightning a great night's sleep, and I pulled myself into my bed. I rolled over and off to La-La-Land I went, having the greatest dreams about Becky and me.

CHAPTER ELEVEN

A GIFT FROM MY HEART

I awoke the next morning, thinking of Becky and decided to buy a gift for her to show her how much I liked her. As my feet hit the floor, I felt that I could take on whatever problems might come my way. I walked over to my closet and set my clothes out after patted Lightning on the head; he tells me that he appreciated what I had done for him yesterday. I walked into the bathroom to get ready to go shopping. As I showered, I thought just what an appropriate gift for Becky would be. I had some money, but I knew that my finances were limited. I thought about asking my dad for an advance on my allowance, but then I would have to explain what it was for, and I did not want to have to answer questions about how I felt about Becky.

As I got out of the shower, I thought that it would be a good idea to see just what I have in my secret stash. When I counted my money, I found that I had saved a total of one hundred and twenty dollars. I thought that I should be able to find something nice for Becky with that amount of cash. Putting on my clothes, I wondered if Becky liked me or if she was just a polite girl. I asked myself if I was setting myself up for a big disappointment, but I was willing to take that chance. I felt that I needed to know now if my ideas were correct.

Today was Saturday, so plenty of stores would be open that sold jewelry.

After I finished dressing, I picked up my money off the bed and placed the bills in my wallet. I walked to the front of the house to the kitchen and found only my mom was there. Lightning was still asleep in the bedroom. I walked over to the table and sat down, Mom immediately placed breakfast in front of me, and I began to eat my pancakes and looking up at her I ask, "Can I talk to you for a minute?" She sat down and folded her hands on the table, waiting for me to speak. She did not say anything, and by her folding her hands, I knew that she was giving me her full attention.

I said, "Mom, please doesn't laugh at me, but I have a crucial question. How do you know that you are really in love?"

She looked at me and said, "That's not a real easy question to answer. But when I was about your age, I had similar questions that ran through my mind. When I asked that same question, my parents just told me that I was too young to know. But all I can say is that I did know how I was feeling at the age of twelve, and I thought that I needed to know for myself. So, I dated the guy I thought I loved and found out that he was not for me. I thought he was the one, but as I said, I had to find out for myself. I will say that no one can tell you who is to be that special one in your life. I am going to tell you that if you think there is a special someone, I think you should do as I did and find out. You are never too young to have girlfriends, Mickey.

I ended up marrying your dad many years later. When I met your father, I felt that your father was the one that I had been looking for all my life. I can say that I knew as soon as I met him at work that he was that special person. And boy was I right, but it took your father all day to realize that I was the one for him. We made friends the first day we met at work. But it took him a little longer to realize what I already knew. All I can say is I am hoping that you get your education out of the way before you allow yourself to get too involved with any girl. But I also know that one can have the best of intentions, but they can get lost fast when it comes to your heart."

I said, "Thanks, Mom, for talking to me and not treating me like a little kid when I tell you the concerns of my heart."

I ate then rose from the table and went back to my room. Lightning was still asleep. But when I walked in, he awoke and went over to his water dish and took a long drink. He came over to me and sat down after a while. Then he started to smile and sent me several thoughts.

"I see that you are overly concerned about whether Becky feels the same way you do. I can say first and foremost that you can never know for sure until you take a chance, my friend. I think you should give her a gift and see what her reaction is."

I sat and pondered his remarks and thought he is right. I finished getting ready to go shopping and find just the right gift. I was finally ready to walk out the door. I patted Lightning on the head and told him, "Thanks."

I went out into the garage, took my new bike, and headed for town. I was preoccupied with my thoughts, so the trip seemed to pass very quickly. I chained up my bike in front of the jewelry store and went inside.

Five people were inside the store. Everyone looked up at me when I walked in, but they all quickly returned to their shopping.

I was brought out of my deep thoughts when the sales clerk asked, "Is there anything I can help you with?"

I know I must have been blushing because my face and neck were hot. But I felt that this was far too important than to give in to my embarrassment now. And so, I pressed on, "I'm here to buy a gift for a girl."

She smiled and asked, "Well, what did you have in mind, young man?"

I told her, "I don't know what I want exactly."

She smiled and asked, "When is her birthday?"

I first said, "I didn't know." But then I remembered the first day of class when I found out that Becky and Biff were twins; I was pretty sure that he had said they were born in the first part of October. I told the sales clerk, "It's toward the beginning of October, but I can't remember the exact date."

The clerk said, "Her birthstones are Tourmaline and Opal. Tourmalines come in many different colors, but pink is the most popular; Opals are white with rainbow fragments that shift and change. There are a lot of shapes to choose from in both neckless and bracelets."

She then took me to the display case on the other end of the store that had a sign hanging over it in big letters "Birthstones." Then she opened the case and brought out several pieces of jewelry and laid them on top of the glass counter on top of a dark blue velvet cloth. And the clerk showed me all the beautiful colors and every kind of ring, necklace, and earring one could imagine.

I just stared at the case and saw one of the pieces of jewelry that seem to jump out at me, a neckless that was the one that I wanted for her. The necklace said just what I wanted to say to Becky. It was small but pretty like her.

It had many small light blue tourmalines that made the neckless glisten and danced as it was turned or twisted, and the light struck it sent light shooting out from all angles. It was a light blue that matched her eyes, and then a small pink tourmaline heart that hung down. I knew that this was what I wanted to give her.

I was a little embarrassed when I found this out because the little tags that had the price on all the jewelry was not visible inside the velvet case. So, I did not find out what the cost was until after I had chosen it. I was ten dollars and fifty cents short of the price.

She seemed to see my embarrassment and to make me feel at ease, she smiled and said, "Just a moment." She walked over to where the store owner was. They talked in low tones.

The owner was smiling as he came and stood in front of me. His smile broadened as he laid the neckless on the counter in front of me.

He asked, "Is this for your girlfriend?" I nodded yes, and he said, "Young man, this is your lucky day. Today is the 50th anniversary of the day our store opened, so I'm going to sell the necklace to you for the money you've given the clerk. And if you will leave it with me, I will engrave it, especially for you. What is the fine young lady's name?" I told him, "Becky." He took a pad of paper from under the counter and wrote that down. He then asked my name; I told him, "Mickey," and he wrote that down too.

He took the necklace, and a twenty from the cash I had given the clerk. He said, "When you give her this gift, give her at least one red rose. You will never regret it. So, when you give this to Becky, and he raised the box holding the neckless, and you top it with the rose, she will know the gift came from your heart."

I looked at the store owner and the clerk as they smiled at me, and then I realized that they were a married couple as she held his hand.

"It will be ready in about an hour because my son is my engraver. He will be here any moment, and I'll get him on this right away."

He jokingly said, "And young man, when in a few years you decide to get her a special ring, doesn't forget us."

I nodded and said, "Thank you very much. And I won't forget!"

I left to go by the florist just a couple of doors down the street. I wanted to find out what a single rose cost. I didn't want to get it now but wanted to wait until I was ready to give Becky both the necklace and the rose.

As I entered the Florist Shop and I found the smell of the flowers was overpowering, and as I looked around the shop, I spotted a cooler in the back that was full of flowers. And when I approached it found that they not only had the red roses on hand but a multitude of other colors as well. I noticed that the price was five dollars for each rose, but a dozen was thirty dollars and fifty cents. I made a mental note now knowing that they had what I wanted.

I had about an hour to kill, and I didn't know how I was going to spend the time. As I was walking along, I looked down the street and saw Becky with her mother. I walked up and greeted them, "Hi, Becky. Hello, Mrs. Beckman."

Becky returned the greeting, "Hi Mickey." Becky's mom echoed, "Hi, Mickey." Her mom sounded sincere and happy.

Then Becky said, "Fancy meeting you down here." Becky's mom asked, "Are you the boy my kids have been talking about?" She extended her hand and said, "I am Becky and Biff's mother. I am so glad to meet you, Mickey. What are you doing down here?"

I said, "I am getting a gift for someone."

Becky asked, "Oh, is someone in your family having a birthday?" She tilted her chin down and looked up at me. The look started a flutter to my stomach. I thought how cute she was. Her actions seemed to say she did indeed care about me. I knew I could be wrong, but I believed that this was no act.

This look was one that I loved to see, and it made my stomach flutter every time.

I asked Becky, "Would you like to hang out for a while? I could take you home on my bike later if you have the free time. We could have a soda or something."

She looked at her mother, "Can I?"

Her mother stopped and asked me, "Your family is coming over for dinner tonight. So why don't you two ride your bike over to your house, then come to our place with your parents?"

Both Becky and I nodded our heads in approval of this plan. And as we turned, I saw her mother smile and say, "You two be gone and enjoy the sunshine, but please be safe!"

Again we both nodded and turned to walk away, and I saw a big grin come over Becky's face as she very naturally took my hand. As she had taken my hand first, I felt even stronger about my thoughts earlier. It felt so good to be holding her hand.

As we walked a little farther, she squeezed my hand and said, "I was so bored at home, and now that you are here with me, I'm delighted! Biff was watching football games, and I didn't want to watch them with him. I'm so happy that I met up with you, Mickey."

She was dressed in a bright yellow dress like she had just gotten out of church, and this was only Saturday. Her beauty caused me to reflect very fast upon what Lightning had told me earlier.

I turned my mind back to Becky. I was just a little uneasy because my palms were starting to sweat.

There were no words to explain how good her statements made me feel and putting to rest even more of the questions that I had had earlier this morning. She does care, but just how much? We entered the café and sat down in one of the booths in the back, trying to get as much privacy as we could.

The waitress came right over and asked if we needed to see a menu. We both shook our heads no. I ordered a coke, and Becky nodded her head to confirm that she wanted a coke too. I added a big order of fries as an afterthought with a lot of catsup.

After ordering, Becky said, "Thanks for asking me out for a coke, I guess this is our first date."

Not wanting to risk losing the moment, I said, "You're welcome, Becky! But you know I'm happy to be here with you as well."

We began talking, and the time flew by so quickly. We had covered everything from our favorite movies to the game of football.

When I rechecked the time, I found that we had been talking for over two hours. It seemed like we sat down just a few minutes ago.

It was then that I remembered the jewelry store and flower shop. I told Becky that I had to use the restroom; she smiled and said, "That's all right because I need to use the little girl's room as well."

The restroom sign hung over the hallway leading off the main floor of the restaurant. We walked back, and as Becky turned into the ladies' room, I quickly walked back to the waitress. I told her that I had a surprise for my girlfriend, and I would be right back, but I didn't want Becky to know that I had stepped out. She nodded that she understood. I walked quickly out of the front door and hurried down the street to pick up the neckless and the rose.

When I returned, I wanted to surprise Becky, so I went around to the back of the restaurant. The waitress opened the back door and whispered, "I saw you coming, so I came back to open the door for you."

I said, "Thanks so much!"

She replied, "No problem at all. I can't wait to see her reaction."

I thanked her and walked to our booth. Becky looked very surprised, which was just what I wanted.

Before I sat down, Becky stood up, and when she saw the rose, she asked, "Is this for me?"

I nodded, yes.

She just stood there looking at me without saying a word.

I thought I had misread her true feelings. But then Becky started to cry. I knew then that I had made the right choice. I needed to give a second thank you to the jewelry store owner and let him know I had followed his advice.

Becky came toward me with such speed that she caught me completely by surprise. I had to pick her up in my arms for balance, or she would have bowled me over.

The fluttering feeling in my stomach was back and, not knowing what else to do, I just held her and relished the moment.

I could hear people around us whispering things, but I didn't care; I was enjoying this moment. I also knew that things between us would never be the same again. Now I'm sure that I love Becky with all my heart.

Finally, she broke free and pushed me back a little, and then she leaned in and placed her lips on mine. I thought that my heart was going to burst because it was beating ever so fast. Kissing Becky felt so good to me.

After what seemed like an eternity, but way too short for me, she moved back and said, "Mickey, no one has ever given me flowers before."

She quickly dropped her chin, looking up at me she softly uttered, "Thank you, Mickey, you have made my day! I thought you were never going to tell me how you felt, and here you are, making me the happiest girl in the world. I've loved you, Mickey, since the first time I saw you playing football. I made my brother promise me that he would introduce us."

I sat down in the booth and pulled her hand so she would sit down beside me.

I then remembered the necklace that I had in my pocket. I reached in and pulled it out and held the box in my open hand. I asked, "Becky, I have been wondering if you would like to be my girlfriend." She looked at me with almost a stunned look on her face and said, "Yes, Mickey, I would love to be your girlfriend. And I want you to know you have made me very happy today." She reached over and gave me a big and long kiss.

I told her, "I love you too. You've made me very happy!"

I handed her the long thin velvet box that held the neckless. After she opened the top, I noticed that the small pink heart had the engraving with her name on one side and my name on the other. It was so beautiful, even with my untrained eye.

"Thank you, Mickey, I will never forget today for as long as I live."

We didn't ride back; we just pushed my bike along. I put my hand on top of hers on the seat while we walked.

I can't remember when time flew by so fast it seemed like it was just seconds before we reached my house. As my house loomed up in front of us, I wondered how my mom and dad were going to take the fact that I had a girlfriend. I also knew that she was the daughter of my father's boss.

CHAPTER TWELVE

MY NEW GIFTS TESTED

Monday morning, I felt like I was on top of the world. The dinner the night before was great, and Becky and I were quite the couple. We did everything together. She moved my dinner plate so that I had sat between her and Biff. I quite enjoyed the evening. I noticed Becky wore the neckless that I gave to her earlier, but no one acted like they had even seen it. So we chatted, and I talked to the twins about everything. When it was almost time to go, Becky made an excuse to go outside, after she asked me if I would like to see her mom's flower garden. She asked Biff if he would like to go too, but he turned her down as he wanted to watch a football game. We walked outside, and Becky immediately grabbed my hand. We walked along holding hands. We just talked and walked some more. I found the time that we were alone together as the most peaceful I could ever remember. I wanted to know everything about her and their family. She summarized her family history, and I soaked it up like a sponge.

As we were walking in the garden, occasionally we would give each other a soft kiss. Once, after we had just kissed, l looked up at the house and saw her father looking out the living room window. Then he closed the shade, and I kept expecting him to come tearing down to the garden. The living room window overlooked the garden, so I knew he saw us kissing. But we weren't doing anything wrong, so I assumed that was why her dad didn't come down to the garden.

I was up at the crack of dawn the next day and went for a run. I was trying to keep in shape to play football. Staying in top shape was the best way to stay competitive. I knew that Biff would be doing many of the same things that I am doing. And we are after the same position on the team: quarterback. One week he would start the game as a quarterback while I would begin the next week as QB. And we had found that the teams that did not play us honest paid dearly because of our double threat. It all boiled down to the fact that both of us could run and catch the ball. As QB, I had the best arm, but Biff was a little faster. So our team was undefeated so far this year. Being first was a big thing because this was the first time this team had ever gone undefeated in the league. It was because of our teamwork that no one seemed to be able to touch us so far. Our coach kept saying, "Since our team is working, we don't need to fix anything."

I had just entered my bedroom after a five-mile run. I pulled out our playbook and had just sat down at my desk to go over the new plays the coach had given us as we left the locker room last practice.

I hadn't had the chance before now to see the new plays. I knew that basically, the new plays would run to look like plays that we'd already run. Doing it this way always made it easy for each player to learn new plays a few days before our next game.

Since this was the last game of the season, I needed to study both the halfback and the quarterback positions.

But when I saw the new plays, I knew that Biff was going to get the call. He had made me the one running the ball and catching the ball the most this week. I could see at a glance which play looked just like another play we had in our playbook already.

The coach had left us notes that no one would expect kids our age pulling off plays this technical, but he stated that he knew that we were more than able to do these successfully. He said that he knew that as a team, everyone had to learn the new plays and see how they folded into the old plays. One of the things the coach did was make our offense was a full audible offense, so we had to know the verbal cues that would allow each player to get to the line, and then the QB would look at the defense utter the play call and off we went. It was such a simple way to run a team. He didn't run a lot of exercises during practice because we spent every day going over the new plays at full speed until we had learned the new plays. The real advantage of an audible offense was twofold; the defense against us had a hard time substituting and therefore were very tired by the end of the game. They were a lot more tired than we were, so in the last half, we just walked away with the game.

We are in Pop Warner Football that had only seven games per season, and we wanted to finish the season undefeated. The other team was also undefeated going into this game, and they wanted to win as much as we did. So, we knew that they would be up for this game as much as we would be. If we happened to lose, I didn't want it to be because of my lack of preparation.

I had started to go over plays the second time, and as I was retracing my steps through both positions when the phone rang. I didn't answer it, as I didn't think it would be for me, because I hadn't received any phone calls since we had moved here. Soon Mom called down the hallway and said, "It's for you, Mickey, it's Becky."

I hurried down to the kitchen, and Mom handed me the phone. She smiled knowingly as she gave me the phone. She walked away, and as she did, she grabbed Rocky by the arm and said, "Please come with me into the living room because Mickey needs some privacy."

Becky and I talked for several minutes when she said, "I need to go now, but I wanted you to know that my dad knows about us going together as boyfriend-girlfriend. He saw the neckless and saw our names on opposite sides of the heart. He told me that he liked you, and he felt that we could continue being a boyfriend-girlfriend as long as we didn't let the relationship get out of hand." She continued, "He went on to say that both of us need to not go too far at such a young age." She continues, "My dad added that he would trust us until he saw a reason to lose that trust."

I felt that the conversation was going great, and I was pleased with what Becky had told me. I was somewhat relieved that our relationship was now out in the open

After we finished talking, I looked at the time and found that we had been on the phone for over an hour. I was so surprised that time moved so fast whenever we talked or were together.

I had just settled back and had my playbook in front of me, and I was just starting to trace my part in each new play for the third time. I was just starting with the reversing my roles in how to play my part at the quarterback position. For some reason, I suddenly felt that I would be the starting quarterback. So, I was just tracing my steps through that end of the plays when I hear my mom's voice again, "Mickey, it's Biff on the phone for you."

When I went down and answered the call, Biff responded with a cheerful voice saying, "Hey, buddy, what is this; I hear that you're going steady with my little sister." Not waiting for an answer, he went on, "When were you going to tell your best buddy? I knew she was hooked on you when all she could talk about was you. She was just waiting for you to wake up and smell the roses, and it looks to me like you have arrived at her destination. She has sure hooked you, and all she has to do is reel you in anytime she wants." He went on, "I couldn't have been happier when she told me and showed her the necklace. That thing is all she can talk about! You both seem to have it bad for each other. And Mickey, I could not be happier for you both, but please don't hurt her. I don't want to lose you as a friend."

Biff paused to let what he said sink in. Then he said again, "I could not be happier for you both!"

Then he asked, "Have you started on the new plays we got at the end of our last practice?"

I answered, "Yes!"

He asked, "Would you like to sit down and go over them at my place?" Then he added, "A certain someone asked me to ask you to come over. And I don't think she gives two hoots about our football plays or even that it is our last game. I think she has other ideas. What do you think?"

He waited for my reply, but I didn't have an answer concerning Becky, so I said, "Yes, I would like to come over and go over the plays together and maybe even walk through them a time or two."

Biff replied, "Great. See you in a few minutes."

I had intentionally sidestepped the issue about Becky, but little did Biff know that her wanting me to come over, was the main reason for agreeing to go over there. My thoughts were going back and forth between the importance of recapping plays and seeing Becky. Friday will be our last game this year, and all hinged upon getting prepared so we could have the title of being number one for the year. Our team has worked hard all season, and to think of coming in less than first would be a real downer to the whole team.

When I knocked on the door to Becky's house, her father answered the door. He smiled down at me and said, "They are in the game room, Mickey, please come in." He reached out, grabbed my hand and shook it firmly. It appeared that he was glad to see me.

I walked into the room and found Biff and Becky watching a TV show. They turned it off as soon as I walked in. Becky rose first when she saw me. She came across the room and hugged me as if she had not seen me for a long time; I can say that it made me feel so good. And right now, I found myself in seventh heaven, my girl and football how could it possibly get better than this.

Biff and I started going over all the plays many times. After that, we went into the backyard and walked through the plays again and again. We both popped questions at each other, and now I felt that we were as ready as we could ever be. I had a great time that night, and I couldn't remember when football, which I love, had ever been this enjoyable either.

Just before I left, they asked me if I went to church, and when I said no, they asked if I would like to go with them. Her dad piped up, "I would be glad to swing by and pick you up in the morning." I agreed because it would give me more time with Becky. I wanted to spend as much time as possible with her.

I was lonely on the bike ride home. And I wished I could've stayed longer at Becky's house.

The Sunday service went well but, I didn't hear much of the minister's sermon because I was too busy holding Becky's hand. I enjoyed the atmosphere at the church, and when we were leaving,

Becky's father stopped and introduced me to the minister. He shook my hand and said, "I'm so glad to see you, Mickey. I hope that you'll come back and see us again. I would like to see your mom and dad here too. Please tell them they're very welcome to join us." Then, almost as an afterthought, he asked, "Do you think your parents would mind if my wife and I came over for a visit? Then I could ask them to attend our services personally." I nodded my head, yes, and he said, "We'll be over on Tuesday afternoon after your father gets off work." He handed me a business card and asked, "Would you hand this to your parents? Please ask them to call me and let me know if Tuesday's visit will work."

I left the church with the card in the pocket of my suit coat, and I was deep in thought about my family as to why had they never been churchgoers. Maybe my mom and dad would like to go, and it was their decision one way or the other. I asked myself why we had never gone to church as a family. I liked going and knew that I would like to attend church together, but maybe there was a reason that they never went.

As we approached the car to leave, there was a cry for help coming from the other side of the church. We all hurried around to the back of the church. There we saw a group of the congregation standing together looking at the ground. All of the families hovered around to see what was going on. As I looked closer, I could a young boy lying on the ground; it appeared he had fallen out of the tree. Another boy was lying right next to the first boy. They both lay motionless on the ground. I saw that the boys' faces were both as white as a sheet. I realized that neither of the boys were breathing.

Someone yelled, "Call 911!" A woman asked, "Can anyone help?" No one answered. I realized that the woman asking for help was the mother of the two boys because they looked just like her.

I looked around again, and no one was coming forward.

She then, with tears streaming down her face, looked up with a pleading look on her face. But still there was no response from the crowd.

I then remembered that according to what Lightning had told me that I was to have the gift of healing in my hands to help others. I decided to try to use that gift to save these two young boys.

I raised my hand and said, "I had some first aid training in school, and I'd like to try to help."

The mother pulled me quickly toward her and, in a pleading, desperate voice, asked, "Will you see what you can do for them?"

A calm came over me and filled my body. I knew that I could help with these two boys. I knelt between both boys and placed one of my hands on one boy's chest while placing the other on the other boy's chest. Then at the same time, I bowed my head as if I were praying. I did this while I did chest compressions like I was starting CPR. I thought it would be easier to explain a miracle of healing as coming from God. After all, hadn't Lightning mentioned the great spirit was at the heart of the gifts I received? I was doing this on the spur of the moment here, and I had only done this one time for Lightning, but as I worked, I could remember just how to do it. And who is to say that this gift was not from God in the first place.

I found as I continued to touch both boys, there was no noise coming from the congregation, not even the children were talking. I found that there was a very soft snapping sound that I was sure no one else could hear. I found upon opening my eyes that it was coming from my hands as I placed them on the two boys. I felt another silent bolt pass on through my hands and out to my fingertips into each boy. I found that the feeling was instead was very soothing to me, and I hoped the boys felt it too.

All at once, both boys took a deep breath at the same time. At once, both boys began breathing on their own. Their mother let out a yell, "It's a miracle, young man, and thank you so very, very much." The look in her eyes was worth it all to me; it was then that a strong feeling of great joy swept through me right down to my very soul.

The feeling that coursed through my mind made me feel outstanding. It wasn't a feeling of pride in the act that made me feel so great; it was just a thankful feeling that I had a gift that let me heal others.

The murmur that went through the crowd was one of total happiness. Everyone wanted to shake my hand, and I liked the feeling that gave me. I looked around and found Becky in the crowd, and I could see that some pride filled her face, as she seemed more than happy with what I had done.

I felt great and wanted to spend some time alone with Becky. But I felt that things would never be the same ever again. I knew that my life would be a lot more complicated, and I was just a twelve-year-old kid.

When we finally got to the car, they were all talking about what had happened at church. I just sat back, holding Becky's hand, and when we arrived at my home, they let me out. Becky's father hurriedly got out of the car and opened my door for me. He extended his hand and shook mine and said, "That was an incredibly wonderful thing you did back at the church. I want you to know just how much it meant to my faith, son." Then he reached out and drew me to him I could see a tear forming in the corner of his eye. He then pushed me out to arm's length and said, "You did your family proud today, young man." He got back into the car, and I waved goodbye as they drove away.

I was walking on air as I entered the house and found Mom, Dad, and Rocky sitting at the kitchen table. All three were staring at me as I entered and sat down. "Well?" Mom asked.

Dad didn't say anything, but he simply nodded toward Mom.

Not knowing what they were asking about, was it the church service or the healing afterward?

So, I just played dumb and asked, "What?"

The phone rang, and I thought that took me off the hook. Mom answered the phone, but my dad asked, "What happened after church today, Mickey? We couldn't wait for you to get home and tell us."

Rocky asked, "What kind of miracle did you do today, Mickey?" He went on to say, "I didn't know that you could do miracles." Then he asked, "Why didn't you do a miracle on me when I fell back in New Jersey and broke my arm playing baseball? It hurt awful, Mickey, and I wish you would have healed me back then!"

I looked at Rocky and said, "I didn't know that I could heal anyone back then, Rocky. I would've done it if I knew I could, and maybe this time was a fluke who knows?" Wanting to open the door to the ESP part of Lightning's and my plan, I added, "You know, Rocky, this only happened after lightning struck me."

Dad and Rocky seemed satisfied with my answer.

Mom came back to the table and asked, "Mickey, what is this all about?"

I looked at her and shrugged my shoulders, but said nothing.

Dad told her what we had been talking about while she was on the phone.

I said, "Just maybe, Mom, it's because now I might have ESP." They all stopped and stared at me; none of them saying anything.

It was Rocky who asked, "What is ESP, Mickey?"

Dad answered him, "It's when some people believe that their minds can do things that supposedly normal people can't do."

I felt that I had answered all their questions and wanted to tell Lightning about the day's happenings. I found him lying on my bed and took him outside to do his business. I knew he hadn't been out of the bedroom most of the day.

As we walked out, he scanned my mind and knew everything in a matter of seconds. He looked up at me and said, "It was so much fun to communicate this way, and I've missed it for such a long time. And we are getting good at it."

I thought, "You have always been able to do this. I'm just catching up."

He told me, "We need to take this to a higher level by practicing thinking deeper thoughts. The purpose of this exercise will be to teach you more about all the gifts that you now have, and the understanding will become harder to forget." So we sat there for about forty-five minutes doing that, and when we stopped, I had learned more about three of my gifts and felt that I knew how to use them.

The next day school was hard for me. I was the talk of the whole school. Everyone knew me and wanted to talk about what had happened; even the teachers stopped me and wanted to talk to get the truth of what happened.

That was how the day went up until noon when the sky fell in. During the lunch hour, there were two media vans out in front of the school. The whole school was ablaze with different ideas of what the media was doing there. Most speculated that it was all about what had happened after church yesterday.

Then I heard that a reporter wanted to talk to me. But the school officials would not let them speak to me without my parent's permission. So, the principal escorted me to his office to wait until my parents could come.

I found out that channel 12 out of Portland, Oregon, was willing to pay my parents ten thousand dollars for an interview with me. Channel six also offered to pay for an interview as well. I thought this was so silly, but then I thought again if I were the one on the other side of this, I would want to know the truth. So yes, I thought I would want to hear it from the person who was involved. My father left work early so he could talk to the media, and when he arrived at school.

Dad took me out in the hallway to speak privately. He asked me, "What do you think about this, Mickey?" I thought for a moment and told my dad that I didn't want to do it. I remembered what Lightning told me about earning money from my gift and that I could lose it if I used it for personal gain.

Dad then said, "If you don't want to do an interview, then I'll take you home."

He took me, and we quietly left by the back door. We hurried to dad's car. When we got home, it was like a circus in front of our house. There were several media vans, maybe even more than had been at the school.

My mom had called the sheriff to keep the people off our property. Dad had the garage door open before we turned into our driveway. He closed the door as soon as we parked inside. We could hear the reporters as they were calling out to us. Dad hugged me as we entered the kitchen and found my mom fretting over all the media interest.

Dad told Mom and me to take a few minutes to settle down. In the meantime, he would see what he could do about the media. I watched from the living room with Rocky as we saw Dad go out onto the front porch. As Dad got ready to speak, I realized Lightning was sitting at my side. He scanned my mind to find out what was happening. I let him know that the problem was I couldn't talk to the media people because of what you had told me about using my gifts to get rewarded. He corrected me by saying, "It would be alright to get money for two reasons. First, they were the ones to offer, and second, they can pay. If you had been the one to have solicited the interview for personal gain, it would not have been okay. But since the news media made the offer, then it would be all right to do the interview and collect the money."

I had to think about it and decide on a game plan. I would need to have a reason for my change of heart. I then walked out to the front door and asked Dad, "Please come in for a minute to talk."

He came in, and I said, "Dad, if they're still willing to pay, I will give the interview if they don't bother me at school or anywhere else afterward. Also, I would be willing to do it as a joint interview for both channels, and they all must have to agree, or there is no deal. We could use the money for my college fund."

Dad motioned for the reporters to come over, and he asked them if they would contribute to Mickey's college fund, that I would be willing to do the interview. The news reporters looked at each other, and without any hesitation, handed my dad a voucher.

Dad came back to where I was standing and asked me if I was ready for this. He told me that they had agreed on a half-hour interview, and each of the stations would be allowed to ask questions for fifteen minutes each. I nodded my head, and the camera crews, and the reporters rushed to enter our house. I was sitting on the hearth of our big fireplace. They came in and immediately started to set up the cameras and the sound systems. I just sat there trying to think about any questions that they may want to ask me. I was trying to think about how I was going to answer those questions without giving away the secret of my gifts that I hold.

Then about the time they were ready, I noticed that Lightning had come to sit at my feet, and him being there made me feel a lot better. I greeted him in our usual way. He told me to relax and think before I answered and that he would be there to help me through this.

They had flipped a coin, and channel six would ask the questions in the first fifteen minutes.

They started with, "Mickey, how did you feel when you reached out and laid hands on the two younger boys? Everyone in the crowd thought the two boys might die. And yet a few minutes later, these same boys got to their feet after you simply had laid hands on them not unlike what Christ in the Bible had done centuries ago."

I paused and listened to Lightning give me his thoughts on the subject. He told me to tell them first that, "I don't want anyone to think I'm putting myself in the same league as Jesus Christ. I am just a simple kid trying to come to grips with a gift that I seem to have received. And who knows that may be the only time it happens. It is the first time for me." I went on to answer the first part of the question, "It made me feel super to have been able to help those little guys."

The second question was, "How does being in the limelight feel to you?"

I paused and then answered, "I'm glad that I was able to help, but this doesn't seem real to me. I don't want this type of limelight as you call; it's not who I am, and it's not what our family needs right now either."

Then the reporter asked me, "How do you like it here? What differences do you find in this place compared to where you lived before?"

I answered after a pause and getting no feedback from Lightning, "I loved it where I came from, and hated leaving my friends. But since moving here, I've made new friends and am now very happy to be here."

The next question was completely unexpected, "I understand Mickey that you have a new girlfriend; do you care to tell the TV audience about the new girl in your life?"

I didn't want to answer, but I did because I wanted the whole world to know that I had someone special in my life, and I wanted Becky to know how proud I was of her. I thought about the problems this might cause her, and I wanted to save her from the press. So, I answered, "You make it sound like I've had lots of girlfriends. She is the only girlfriend I've ever had, and we're going steady, but I don't want you to bother her. Please remember we're only twelve-years-old!"

They must have sensed that it upset me because they turned from that line of questioning. The reporter asked, "Your vet told us that you survived after being struck by lightning because a dog saved your life. Is that true?"

I answered, "Yes, that;s true as far as we know. I was unconscious, and when I came around, I found Lightning lying on top of me. I have two perfect pawprints on my chest that exactly match the dog's paws. According to the Vet, he thinks that maybe the dog sensed that lightning was about to strike, and he willingly placed himself in harm's way to save me, but we will never know for sure." I rose and pulled up my shirt, and my burn scars were there as plain as day. After that, I called Lightning's name, and he stood up. I then patted my chest, and Lightning jumped up, putting his front paws on my shoulders. I knew that the reporters could see the damage along with the path the lightning had traveled down Lightning's back and tail. I let Lightning go, and he laid back down. I sat down again.

"As I said, we figured in that split second when Lightning knocked me off my feet since I was in contact with the tree and him, so I was not in contact with the ground. He landed on top of me, and it took him several hours to come around. I will always believe that Lightning saved my life."

My father came to stand beside me and said, "I think that's enough for now. Please pack up your cameras and head toward the door. I believe we've fulfilled our part of the interview deal. We need to get back to some proximity of normal for us right now." With that, my dad opened the front door and ushered them out of our home.

One of the reporters handed my dad a card and said, "Would you please keep this? You should be prepared to have more people try to get your in-depth story and requests for interviews on many of the TV talk shows as well. You haven't seen what they'll do to get more of this story. If you would like an agent, I'd like to put in for the job. My name is Mike, and I know everyone in the industry. I'll move here to Ridgefield if you sign with me, and you'll be my first and only client. I can make your family very wealthy."

My father took his card and said, "I don't think we'll need your services because I hope my family can go back to the way things were before tonight."

Mike said, "Good luck with that because as your family is not only news but positive good news, and we are always trying to find positive news stories. You see, Mr. Hunter, they are much harder to find, while sex and violence are always easy to come by. While good clean, positive news is at a premium these days. If I can help in any way, please get in touch with me. I will treat you right and always with respect."

When the crowd cleared out, we all collapsed into the furniture to take a few moments to recoup our energy.

Dad said, "I hope this is the end of this mess, but we'll have to see. It's time for bed; we should turn in so we can get up and start tomorrow with, hopefully, a little less stress in our lives. But I don't believe that's going to be the case here, guys. Like the reporter said, this is too good of a story, and they will want to play it to the hilt. So, see you for breakfast in the morning."

The next morning I got out of bed reluctantly because I didn't get a lot of sleep last night. I kept thinking about Becky one moment, and about the media intrusion the next. My only hope was that I could stay awake in class today because the football league rules were very strict about missing classes. One missed class unexcused meant that you couldn't play in the first quarter of the next game. If you missed a second unexcused missed class, you were unable to play for the first half. The rules were to make sure school came first, even at a young age.

I arrived at school early, because I wanted to go unnoticed as much as possible. I could not wait to see Becky and find out if she had seen the interview.

I sat on the bench outside next to the playground. I was nice and warm in my heavy jacket. It seemed like only seconds has passed, but Becky found me fast asleep on the bench. I awoke with Becky was pulling on my jacket sleeve. When I looked up and saw her beautiful smile and the neckless with the heart dangling from her neck, I was happy. I clasped her hand and asked her if she had seen the interview, and she nodded yes. I felt like she was troubled about something, and I couldn't tell what it could be.

I never saw Becky upset before now. It hit me then that perhaps her father was concerned after seeing the interview last night.

Becky said, "My dad thinks we need to cool it for a while and let things sort themselves out. He thinks you are a great guy, and he has nothing against our going steady after things get back on an even keel again." I could tell she had been crying and saw she still genuinely loves me. But I could see just how upset she was about slowing things down for a while. I could feel just how torn she was between what she felt for me and trying to do what her father wanted. I now know that I needed to relieve her of that feeling of guilt.

I waited a few moments then said, "I think that until this all blows over, we shouldn't be so close." She looked at me and asked, "Do you want to break up with me or just spend less time together for a while?"

I told her, "No way am I trying to break up with you, but I'm concerned about you getting dragged into this media mess."

She smiled at me and said, "My daddy said almost the same thing." She then took the neckless off and placed it in her purse. She said that she would put it away at home until the coast was clear.

She stood up, kissed me, and then abruptly walked away. I think she was crying, but I wasn't sure. But I know how I felt within myself, it was one of the saddest days in my life.

Thinking about yesterday, and I wondered how one day could put you on top of the world, and the very next day, you could be lower than a centipede with fallen arches. I watched as Becky turned the corner, and she never looked back. After school, I went straight home thinking about taking a nap to catch up on some sleep.

As I entered the house, I could hear Mom's frustrated voice. She was talking to someone on the phone. After she hung up, she said, "The phone calls started a little after ten this morning, and they have not let up all day." I told her I was sorry about the trouble. Then I headed to my bedroom to take that nap.

When Dad got home from work, Mom called me to come downstairs. We sat down at the table, and Mom said, " The phone has been ringing all day long. I don't know what to do. What do you think we should do? I'm at my wit's end! I can't keep this up. I think about just unplugging the phone, but then I am worried that one of you will need me, and I wouldn't be able to answer." She paused for a second then said, "The callers wanted everything from Mickey being a sponsor for a new type of tennis shoes to very well paying interviews on all the daytime and nighttime TV talk shows."

My father said, "If we kept turning them down and there being so many of them, I can't keep up with everything coming at us every day either. Mickey, I don't think this is going to stop just like the news guy said it would, until you go on some of these shows, because when we refuse, it becomes more enticing for them." I nodded my approval. Mom and Rocky nodded their approval too.

I told him, "Anything to get us back to normal." But my dad said, "Son, I don't think that it will ever be back to the way it was because you are a hero in other's eyes, and I don't see that changing anytime soon."

Then Mom and Dad discussed between themselves if we should stay home from school for a few days or perhaps even longer. They told us that they wanted to try and protect me as much as possible. They could not make up their minds one way or the other, so they finally asked us what we wanted to do.

I told them, "Even if I stay home, I'll have to answer the same questions when I do go back to school."

Rocky shrugged his shoulders and said, "I don't know!"

Dad looked at me and said, "Son, I think that's a good idea." I looked at my mom, and she shrugged her shoulders and then nodded yes.

Dad said, "Well, then tomorrow, you will go back to school and try to make the best of it while I get in touch with the reporter and hire him as our agent."

The next day, I arrived at school early, and when I walked up to the school, I noticed all the media people were gone. The only cars in the parking lot were the teachers' cars that were usually there.

I sat down on a bench and waited for Becky to arrive because she was the main reason that I wanted to go back to school. The students started to arrive, and I saw her as she walked across the playground. I thought Becky looked lovely in a knee-length white skirt with a blouse that was bright yellow. Her hair was pulled back in a ponytail that streamed do her back. She was so incredibly beautiful. Yellow tennis shoes topped off her outfit, and she walked like she was floating on air.

The day was already looking brighter than yesterday, and this good-looking young lady was headed my way. I held my breath as she came closer because I was afraid that she might disappear.

Then I saw the camera crew was coming in behind her, so I stood up and yelled at Becky, "Don't come near me I don't have any more to do with you, please stay away from me." I jumped up and walked very fast away from her. I saw Becky pause, and she looked stunned. She then turned and started to walk in the opposite direction from where I was disappearing; she was going right back through all the crowd of news people.

I wanted to yell at the top of my lungs to stop and come back, that I didn't mean it. But instead I just kept walking because I wanted to protect Becky from the TV reporters.

The TV crews stopped and looked at each other like they didn't know who they wanted to follow, Becky or me.

I heard a stern voice coming from the opposite side of the courtyard, but I couldn't see who was speaking. But then the speaker walked into my view, and I saw that it was the sheriff and two of his deputies. As they came into view, I could tell from his actions that he was upset. He asked, "What in the world are you folks doing here?" Not waiting for a response, he went on, "Get off this property, and if I see you here again uninvited, I will arrest all of you. This school is private property, and you folks are interrupting the function of this school now get!"

He turned to his deputies and said, "If you see them on this school grounds again, arrest them." I watched as the reporters turned around and walked out the same way they had come from earlier.

I ran to where I thought that Becky might be now. But when I got to the courtyard, I couldn't see her anywhere. That was when I saw a glimpse of something or someone out of the corner of my eye, and it was so fast that I did not even have time to react. The blow struck me on the side of my face and sent me reeling. I fell, but I jumped up and, without even thinking, I hit back with a force that sent my attacker flying. When I came to my senses, I saw Biff lying on the ground, knocked out. Then I remembered Lightning had warned me that I could only use the gift of added strength when there was a real threat.

I then knew that I had brought that strength to bear when I hit Biff. The problem was Biff was lying there motionless, and it seemed that he was having trouble breathing. Then I realized that he was not having a difficult time breathing; he wasn't breathing at all. I panicked and tried to get to Biff. But a sheriff's deputy grabbed my arm to stop me. I tried to push him away so I could help Biff. I said, "I want to get to him. He's my best friend."

The deputy said, "You helped him quite enough; you hurt him quite badly." It was then I knew he hadn't seen the first part of the fight where Biff had hit me first, and I was just defending myself. I knew that I needed to get to him so I can heal him, the rest we can sort out later.

The sheriff came around the corner of the building and immediately saw the deputy holding my arm, and, without saying anything, he took my other arm, and they started to remove me from the courtyard.

I screamed out, "Let me help him; he needs my help," and the deputy repeated, "You have helped that boy quite enough for now."

I looked back down at Biff as they were pulling me toward the parking lot. I could see that he was still not breathing. I pulled to get free, and they just gripped me harder and kept taking me away. I said again, "I need to help him, or he's going to die."

They stopped for a second and said, "Paramedics are on the way; they can help him better than you." I tried to stop them, but it didn't work. Then I willed the change in my strength again, but this time, I was controlling the level.

As my arms came to their full strength, I had flung them several feet away, onto a grassy area rather than the asphalt of the parking lot. I was able to return to Biff and render the aid he so desperately needed. I saw he was still lying where he had fallen and still wasn't breathing.

I reached down and placed my hands on him, and I immediately felt the healing flow through my arms to my hands and then exit out of my fingers,

He immediately let out a cough and tried to get up. I started to cry as I held him to my chest. Biff rolled away from me a short way, looking back at me, and said, "Dang you, Mickey, what happened?"

I heard Becky's voice, "I know what happened because I saw it. You hit Mickey, and he hit you back. It looked like he hit you harder than you hit him."

Trying to downplay the situation, I said, "I've heard that when one's adrenalin is running hard that sometimes they can do superhuman things. Are you all right, Biff?" Biff said, "Yeah, I'm alright." I added, "I'm so sorry I hit you. Please forgive me, but why did you do that in the first place?"

He looked at me and then at Becky and said, "I thought you hurt my little sister."

I looked at Becky and said, "I yelled at you because the reporters were coming up behind you. I was trying to protect you from them! As soon as the sheriff's deputies removed the reporters from the schoolyard, I was coming to find you."

Biff looked at me and said, "I'm so sorry that I overreacted."

Becky ran over to where I was and threw her arms around my neck and kissed me on the lips. She said, "I'm so sorry that I ever doubted you, Mickey, I will never do that again!"

I looked back to where the deputies were. They had regained their wits and headed toward me. The first deputy asked, "How did you do that, young man?" Without even letting me answer, he asked, "Just how were you able to toss us that far." He went on jokingly, "Whatever you are eating young man, I want some of it."

I answered, "I guess that when the adrenalin rush hit me, it must've allowed me to call upon my superhuman strength. That's the only answer I have, Sir. When I saw that my friend Biff was going to die, I felt this added strength. I thought you weren't listening to me."

As they walked away, the sheriff said, "You guys make sure to keep it peaceful for the rest of the day."

I let out a sigh of relief and realized this was another hectic day in my life. I hugged Becky and told her, "I'm so sorry I hurt your feelings, I wish there had been a better way. It was the only thing that I could think of at that split second. I thought I needed to take care of this before it got any more out of hand." I told her, "I will have to see you guys later."

I hugged her and walked away.

CHAPTER THIRTEEN

TRYING TO FIND
NORMAL AGAIN

I entered my dad's office, and the first thing he asked was, "Why aren't you in school? Is everything alright?"

I told him about the incident at school, then said, "They aren't going to stop until they get all their questions answered. Do you know of any way to stop this mess?"

He shook his head and said, "I don't have a clue!"

"Well, Dad, I want to run something by you and see what you think. I think we should get in contact with the media guy who gave you his card and ask him to help us. It seems to me that each reporter is trying to get an exclusive. I think we'll be under a bombardment until we allow the news media to get to know us as a family. Then I believe they will tire of this and leave us alone."

Dad didn't say a word for what seemed like quite a long time. Then he said, "I think that's an excellent idea, but we need to run it by your mother to see if she likes the idea; otherwise, she'll be upset that we hadn't kept her in the loop. You know as well as anyone how your mother is when she wants to protect her kids. So I think we need to go through this as a family."

I left and took the bus back home. When I got home and passed the place where this had all begun, a smile crossed my lips as I remembered I first thought Lightning was a bear. I stopped long enough to scan the place where I had been under the tree. I looked up at the tree and for the first time since the incident. I saw where the lightning had cut a blaze out of the tree bark. It was about four inches wide and stopped about five feet from the ground. It was then that I knew for a fact that Lightning saved my life.

I walked up the hill, remembering that evening, and it was now evident in my mind as to just how it had happened. Smiling, I remembered how things changed in my mom's and dad's eyes when they realized that Lightning had saved my life.

I walked into the house and went directly to my room to let Lightning know where things were probably headed. I also wanted to discuss what I could or could not do with my gifts because I was afraid of losing them after what happened earlier that day.

As I sat down, Lightning scanned my mind in a few seconds, and that brought him up to speed quickly on all the happenings up to date.

I bounced ideas off him about trying to get back to normal. He agreed with the game plan, and said that it was all right to do this as long as I didn't charge for the interviews, but let the networks give me what they thought it was worth to them. Also, tell your agent what can and cannot be said.

Life moved very quickly after Dad met with Mike, the agent. Mike set up a two-week tour of interviews with all the major TV talk shows, and some radio shows too. We went on the road within days of our decision to work with the media.

When we started on the tour, it moved along quickly, and it felt like we were in neverending motion. When I found the two weeks were over and we returned home, I was so very, very glad to see our house again.

Upon arrival, I discovered that all I wanted to do was go over and see Biff and Becky. But down deep, I knew that it was Becky that I wanted to see the most, and I just wanted to spend some quiet time with her.

But I was so exhausted that I felt I could sleep for a week, to catch up on the sleep I had lost in the flash travel arranged for us.

When I arrived back home, the tiredness won out, and I passed on supper and went down the hallway, asking, "Please not disturb me unless it is Becky who calls, because I am so tired."

Both my dad and mom nodded their heads in approval. So off I went to claim the rest that I felt I so desperately needed.

I heard the alarm going off, and as I opened my eyes, I saw daylight. I then spotted Lightning asleep on his bed and knew that I was home.

My question was just what will happen now with Becky, Lightning, and I.

The next morning, when I arrived at Becky's and Biff's place, no one was home, so I left a note and peddled back home on my birthday bike.

I knew there were so many things that were still unanswered. The main one was to find out what Lightning could tell me about the additional gifts he had mentioned. This question soon came to the surface, and it was starting to bug me.

I felt a strong urge to find out, but I understood the big dog needed rest. I knew that my impatience must be silenced for right now. I knew that I needed to get rest, and I knew the big dog needed rest as well. When Lightning woke up, I had a ton of questions to ask him.

I also wondered what would happen with Becky, Biff, and me in the future.

THE END
(OR WAS THIS JUST THE BEGINNING)

Printed in the United States
By Bookmasters